哈福

哈福

Hello~

英語聽力
Listening Comprehension
滿分特訓

哇，聽英文 更清楚了！

一考再考的聽力測驗題庫
總整理 & 試題解答與分析

施銘瑋／主編
Craig Sorenson／著
吳佳燕／譯

哈福

六十分鐘滿分特訓‧英語聽力大晉級！

學英語，聽、說、讀、寫四大基本能力最重要。除了要多讀多看，聽力更是其中一項大工程。各種的英語檢定考試，聽力測驗都可說是成敗關鍵，要勝過別人，除了閱讀與寫作功力要紮實，聽的功力更得爐火純青。為了專攻聽力，讓自己實力大晉級，只要六十分鐘，Ready！Go！

本書特聘專攻各種英語考題名師為讀者編寫，猜題和命中率高，內容包括短文試題、會話試題與圖畫試題三部分。短文內容多元、有趣，文章富啟發與專業 ，並針對各英語聽力測驗常考的問法、主題、方向歸納精編測驗題，各單元測驗重點清晰有條理，七篇精選短文讓您聽力馬上增強三成功力！

會話試題包括九則精彩實況對話，與特選題型，情節發展自然，句型實用，完成練習後，聽力再加四成！

圖畫試題包括七個精心設計的看圖辨義單元題，讓您增進聽力同時提升「聽力測驗」應試實力！十成功力一次累積，萬試亨通，所向無敵！

本聽力測驗特別收錄答題技巧大公開與詳盡的解答分析，是您增進聽力的最大秘密武器。跟著六十分鐘的反覆磨練，聽力絕對過人！

英語聽力滿分特訓使用須知：

迫不期待想提升英聽實力的您，別著急！先看看本書使用須知，搭配最逼真的實戰MP3，與測驗後的檢討分析，您的實力才會真正提升！

本書首先為您精心整理出「Test Tips應試小秘訣」，請先仔細讀過每個條列重點、提示、注意事項等，這些要點都是可以幫助您有效應考的重要訣竅喔！

準備好了嗎？在翻開試題冊的同時，專業出題與猜題名老師會在MP3中，再次以英文提醒您務必先讀過「Test Tips應試小秘訣」。

接下來便是真槍實彈的考試時間了！三階段的題型考試，題目說明都是以英文呈現，不會印在題目冊上，這是為了幫助您習慣各項聽力考試時的考場實況。將來若您參加任何一項國際級的英語考試，這一小小訓練將會是您成功的一大步。

本書使用方法

第一部分「短文試題」，出題與猜題名師會把課文朗讀兩遍。第一遍用正常速度，第二遍速度會略為放慢，同時文章重點部份會加強語氣。最後老師會唸出測驗題目，請注意，問題只播出一遍。請在聽完問題後，迅速地選出正確答案。每題約有十秒的間隔。

第二部分「對話試題」，出題與猜題名老師會用最道地、最逼真的語調與口氣唸出一段對話。對話以正常速度進行，並重複兩遍。最後老師會唸出測驗題目，請注意，題目也只唸一遍。請把握時間快速作答。

第三部分「圖畫試題」，請先看圖片。出題與猜題名師會用正常速度唸出測驗題目與選項。題目與選項都唸兩遍，建議您在聽第一遍時，就快速刪選掉不可能的答案；聽第二遍時，才能遊刃有餘地再次確認答案是否正確。

共三部分試題，考試時間約60分鐘。請完全遵循CD的速度應試，才能達到增加聽力最佳效果！

解答與分析部分：特別精心整理的解答與分析區，除了提供答題技巧與實用範例補充外，更將課文、對話重點用字型突顯出來，讓您省略畫重點的步驟，聽力或閱讀都能一次抓到重點！

編者 謹識

CONTENTS

Chapter 3 Answers and Analyses 解答&解析

Chapter 4 Appendix 附錄

Chapter

1

Listening Skill
聽力應試秘笈

Test Tips 應試小祕訣

❶ **刪去法**：先刪除不可能的選項，這樣可以快速找到正確答案。記住，有時候刪除錯誤的答案，比尋找正確的答案要來得容易。

❷ **障眼法**：試題所提供的資訊，通常會多於回答問題所需的資訊。不要被多餘的訊息給愚弄了！

❸ **小心陷阱**：如果選項包含了幾個句子成分，你得逐項閱讀每個部分才行。確認全部正確才可選擇，只有其中一個句子成分是正確的選項千萬不要選。

❹ **略去非關鍵字**：記得，"has", "the"和"in"這些細微的字常常是無關緊要的！它們既不是關鍵字，也非答題的重點，不要浪費時間記。

❺ **看清答案選項**：當選項是複合句時，要仔細查看每個成分，這樣對答題會有相當大的幫助。

❻ **注意代名詞**：如果一篇對話裡用了許多代名詞，那麼要仔細聽，以便記得代名詞代替哪個名詞，這通常是考題關鍵。

❼ **留意相關提示**：有時候答案並沒有直接陳述出來，這時，你必須尋找文中的相關提示，並利用一點小常識找出答案。

❽ **小心多重字意**：許多英文單字都有多種意義。練習使用這些字詞在不同場合時的意思，尤其要注意，測試時千萬不要混淆了。

❾ **把直述句改成問句**：答句通常都是以直述的方式寫成。倘若你先把直述句改成問句，要找出正確的答案也許就比較容易了。

❿ **為難字解套**：善加利用文中的提示，有助於了解文中的難字部份。文中透露的訊息，不論是單字或片語，皆有助於了解句子的意思，即使並不是所有單字你都認識。

⓫ **小差異露玄機** ：如果你發現所有的選項大致上都一樣。只有一點不同，那麼要注意這些小小的差異之處。

⓬ **用替身逼出本尊**：有時答案的選項可能會故意令人混淆。將這些選項找替代字或改寫成更清楚的型態，將有助於找出正確答案。

- He that can't endure the bad will not live to see the good. （無法撐過苦境，無法看到美地。）

- He who risks nothing gains nothing. （不入虎穴，焉得虎子。）

- No cross, no crown. （沒有痛苦十字架，哪來榮耀冠冕。）

- Nothing ventured nothing gained. （無冒險無所獲。／不入虎穴，焉得虎子。）

- Pleasure comes through toil. （苦盡甘來。）

Chapter

2

The Test is Coming

測驗題庫

Look at all of the questions and Test Tips before you read or listen to the passage. On any test you should always read the questions first!

Part ❶ Essay Question 短文試題

02 Text 1 Dodo

 Question

A. Because of the strange things it ate.

B. Because it could fly very fast.

C. Because the dodo killed many sailors.

D. Because the dodo looked very strange.

Answer see page 36

Text 2 Announcer

Question

❶ A. The slowest runner is from France and the fastest runner is from England.

   B. The fastest runner is from India and the slowest runner is from England.

   C. The slowest runner is from India and the fastest runner is from France.

   D. The fastest runner is from India and the slowest runner is from France.

❷ A. The English runner is faster than the French runner and the Indian runner.

   B. The French runner is faster than the Indian runner but slower than the English runner.

   C. The Indian runner is slower than the French runner but faster than the English runner.

   D. The French and Indian runners are both faster than the English runner.

Text 3 Harvard ■ ■ ■ ■ ■ ■ ■ ■ ■ ■ ■

 Question

❶ A. Because John Harvard was the first student at this school.

B. Because John Harvard was the first teacher at this school.

C. Because John Harvard gave books and land to the school.

D. Because John Harvard first let women attend the school.

❷ A. It is now open to more people from many countries.

B. Now it is much smaller than when it first began.

C. It is now only open to people from Boston.

D. Now only people related to politicians can attend.

Answer see page 44

Text 4 Desk+Book ■ ▪ ■ ▪ ■ ▪ ■ ▪ ■ ▪ ■

 Question

❶ A. Because she wanted to borrow a comic book.

B. Because she wanted to look at her desk.

C. Because she wanted to help Lisa work.

D. Because she wanted to give Lisa a book.

❷ A. The comic book was on the desk.

B. The comic book was behind the desk.

C. The comic book was under the desk.

D. The comic book was inside the desk.

- Something is better than nothing.
  （聊勝於無。）

 Answer see page 48

15

Text 5 Chair-speech ■ ■ ■ ■ ■ ■ ■ ■ ■ ■

Question

❶ A. a baseball player

B. the person who bought a chair

C. the boss of the chair company

D. a worker in the chair company

❷ A. Because the company has been successful and has earned more money.

B. Because the company needs to earn more money so the employees must all work harder.

C. Because too many employees have been going to baseball games instead of going to work.

D. Because the employees can go to baseball games instead of going on vacation.

❸ A. They will meet at 7 pm on Saturday evening.

B. They will be meeting after the game on Saturday.

C. They will all go together to the parking lot after work.

D. They will be meeting at 6:30 pm on Saturday.

Answer   see page 52

Text 6 Pisa ■ ■ ■ ■ ■ ■ ■ ■ ■ ■ ■ ■ ■ ■

 Question

❶ A. Because it was built so long ago using very old stones.

  B. Because it doesn't stand straight, but leans to one side.

  C. Because it was mostly completed in the 1300's in Italy.

  D. Because it is one of the tallest buildings in the world.

❷ A. They dug a hole around the bottom of the tower.

  B. They added more stones to the tall side of the tower.

  C. They added more stones to the short side of the tower.

  D. They finished all eight stories before it began to lean.

❸ A. Although the tower is not straight, builders have never attempted to make it straighter.

B. Because the tower is not straight, builders have tried several times to make it straighter.

C. The tower stood straight for a long time, but has only recently begun to lean to one side.

D. In the past 600 years, the tower has slowly become straighter and straighter.

• Talking mends no holes.
（空談無益。）

Answer　see page 57

1 A. They've allowed people to make more garbage.

B. They've made plastic bags illegal.

C. They've made people use and throw away fewer plastic bags.

D. They've solved the problem of having too much garbage.

2 A. They decided never to use plastic bags.

B. They decided to make people pay for plastic bags.

C. They decided to give everyone plastic bags.

D. They decided that plastic bags are not a problem.

Part ❷ Dialogue Question 對話試題

 Dialogue 1 Haircut ■ ▯ ■ ▯ ■ ▯ ■ ▯ ■ ▯ ■ ▯

 Question

    A. She is playing a game.

    B. She is cutting some papers.

    C. She is getting her hair cut.

    D. She is talking to a doctor.

Dialogue 2 Borrow ■ ▯ ■ ▯ ■ ▯ ■ ▯ ■ ▯ ■ ▯

 Question

    A. He doesn't want to use Mary's dictionary.

    B. He doesn't want to lend Mary his diction-
       ary.

    C. He doesn't want to buy a new dictionary.

    D. He doesn't want to borrow a dictionary.

Answer see page 68

Dialogue 3 Cake ■ ■ ■ ■ ■ ■ ■ ■ ■ ■ ■

 Question

❶ A. Jerry made the cake.

B. Sally made the cake.

C. Jerry's mother made the cake.

D. Sally's mother made the cake.

❷ A. He thinks it's not very sweet and doesn't taste good.

B. He thinks it's very sweet and doesn't taste good.

C. He thinks it's not very sweet and tastes very good.

D. He thinks it's very sweet and tastes very good.

Chapter **2**

• Never do things by halves.
(做事切莫半途而廢。)

 Answer see page 74 ㉑

12 Dialogue 4 Bathroom ■ ■ ■ ■ ■ ■ ■ ■ ■ ■ ■

 Question

A. The bathroom is on the third floor across from the camera store.

B. The bathroom is on the third floor next to the camera store.

C. The bathroom is on the fourth floor across from the camera store.

D. The bathroom is on the fourth floor next to the camera store.

13 Dialogue 5 Pronoun ■ ■ ■ ■ ■ ■ ■ ■ ■ ■ ■

 Question

A. Joe

B. Mrs. Whitefield

C. Both Joe and Mrs. Whitefield

D. Neither Joe nor Mrs. Whitefield

Answer see page 77

Dialogue 6 Cop TV ■ ■ ■ ■ ■ ■ ■ ■ ■ ■

 Question

❶ A. near their home

B. on a television show

C. next to a newspaper

D. all of the above

❷ A. Because the police car could not drive fast enough.

B. Because the police car was driving fast and crashed into a tree.

C. Because the other car was always right behind the police car.

D. Because the other car was not driving as fast as the police car.

• **There are many ways to fame.**
（行行出狀元。）

15 Dialogue 7 Directions ■ ■ ■ ■ ■ ■ ■ ■ ■ ■

 Question

❶ A. The man is driving a car and listening to the radio.

   B. The man is walking on the street and eating.

   C. The man is driving a car and talking to the woman.

   D. The man is walking on the street and looking for the park.

❷ A. directly

   B. wrong

   C. left

   D. correct

• Human effort can achieve anything.
   （事在人為。）

Answer　see page 88

Dialogue 8 Reservations ■ ■ ■ ■ ■ ■ ■ ■ ■

Question

❶ A. Because she wants to know where the restaurant is located.

B. Because she wants to know the name of the restaurant.

C. Because she wants to know how large the restaurant is.

D. Because she wants to know what kind of food the restaurant has.

❷ A. The restaurant requires reservations for very large groups of people.

B. The restaurant does not require reservations, but they are recommended for weekends.

C. The restaurant requires reservations for every day of the week.

D. The restaurant recommends reservations for weekdays, but they are not required for weekends.

Chapter **2**

 Answer   see page 94   25

Dialogue 9 Coffee ■ ■ ■ ■ ■ ■ ■ ■ ■ ■

 Question

❶ A. In a police station.

B. In a coffee shop.

C. In a farmhouse.

D. In a flower store.

❷ A. He would like to hurry up and go and sit down.

B. He would like the other man to go away.

C. He would like to take the other man to go somewhere.

D. He would like to take his drinks out of the store.

• Success belongs to the persevering.
（勝利屬於不屈不撓的人。）

Part ❸ Picture Question 圖畫試題

18 ## Picture 1 Bookstore

Question

1. Ⓐ Ⓑ Ⓒ Ⓓ
2. Ⓐ Ⓑ Ⓒ Ⓓ

Answer see page 105

19 **Picture 2 Pie Chart**

  Question

1. Ⓐ Ⓑ Ⓒ Ⓓ

2. Ⓐ Ⓑ Ⓒ Ⓓ

Jeff's Monthly Expenses

20% School Supplies

25% Food and Drinks

10% Clothes

10% Bus Fare

35% Computer Games

Answer see page 108

20 **Picture 3 Race Time**

 Question

Ⓐ Ⓑ Ⓒ Ⓓ

Two Mile Race Finish Times

Answer **see page 111**

21 **Picture 4 Weather**

 Question

1. Ⓐ   Ⓑ   Ⓒ   Ⓓ

2. Ⓐ   Ⓑ   Ⓒ   Ⓓ

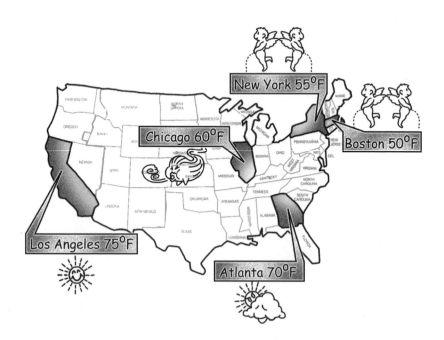

☞ Answer   see page 114

22 **Picture 5 Tall+Book**

 Question

1. Ⓐ Ⓑ Ⓒ Ⓓ
2. Ⓐ Ⓑ Ⓒ Ⓓ

Daniel   Monica   Charles   Henry

Chapter **2**

Answer see page 118

Picture 6 Map

 Question

1. Ⓐ Ⓑ Ⓒ Ⓓ
2. Ⓐ Ⓑ Ⓒ Ⓓ

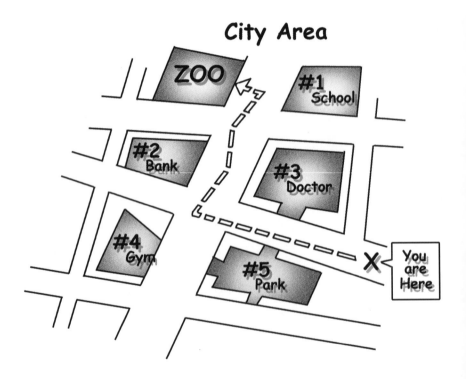

City Area

ZOO

#1 School

#2 Bank

#3 Doctor

#4 Gym

#5 Park

You are Here

Answer see page 121

Picture 7 Tim's Day

 Question

1. Ⓐ Ⓑ Ⓒ Ⓓ
2. Ⓐ Ⓑ Ⓒ Ⓓ

TiM's Morning Schedule

Answer see page 126

- Nothing is impossible for a willing heart.

  （天下無難事，只怕有心人。）

- Nothing in the world is difficult for one who sets his mind to it.

  （專心去做，天下就沒有難事。）

- No pleasure without pain.

  （沒有苦就沒有樂。）

- Human effort can achieve anything.

  （事在人為。）

- Rome was not built in a day.

  （羅馬不是一天造成的。）

- Feather by feather the goose is plucked.

  （一根一根的拔毛，鵝毛也能被拔光。）

- Every little helps.

  （一點一滴都有用。）

- Every little makes a mickle.

  （集腋成裘，積少成多。）

Chapter

3

Answers and Analyses

解答 & 解析

Look at all of the questions and Test Tips before you read or listen to the passage. On any test you should always read the questions first!

請在作答前先看過"應試小秘訣"以利答題。正式作答時，可先看問題選項或圖文，以便更加理解問題。

Part ❶ Essay Question 短文試題

This section include 7 essays, each essay has 1~3 questions. Please listen to the CD and choose to the correct answers, the texts will be read twice.

本單元包含七篇短文，每篇有個一至三個問題，每題會唸兩遍，請聽CD作答，選出正確答案。

Text 1 Dodo ■ ■ ■ ■ ■ ■ ■ ■ ■ ■ ■ ■

史前巨鳥

Have you ever heard of a bird called the dodo? This short, fat bird was first seen by

European sailors on several islands far out in the Indian Ocean. It was a very strange bird, with yellow legs, a black and red face, and a very round body. The dodo was an animal that people didn't discover until the 1500's, yet sadly, the last dodo died less than 200 years later. Why did they all die so quickly? Because the dodo couldn't fly and the sailors quickly killed them all for food.

　　你聽過「多多鳥」嗎？這種又小又肥的鳥類，是由一些歐洲水手首先在印度洋的幾個島嶼上發現的。它是一種相當奇怪的鳥類，有著黃色的腳、黑紅相間的臉、以及圓圓的身體。這種史前巨鳥一直到十六世紀才被人類發現，但很不幸地，不到兩百年之後，最後一隻巨鳥就死掉了。它們為何如此快速地滅絕呢？那是因為史前巨鳥不會飛行，因此水手輕易地就能把牠們抓來吃。

Question and Test Tip Section

<u>D</u> ❶ **Why is the dodo called "a strange bird"?**
「多多鳥」何以被稱為是一種奇怪的鳥類？

A. Because of the strange things it ate.
因為它吃的東西很奇怪。

B. Because it could fly very fast.
因為它能夠飛得很快。

C. Because the dodo killed many sailors.
因為多多鳥殺死很多水手。

D. Because the dodo looked very strange.
因為多多鳥長相很奇特。

解答分析

你看到這個問題當中的關鍵字了嗎？這些關鍵字是「為什麼」、「人們」、「思考」和「奇怪的」。記住："why"是一個疑問詞，需要一個理由來作為答案。這就是為什麼每一個答項都由「因為」作為開頭了。「因為」這個字總是用來作為引介某事物的原因。

記住，在聆聽短文以前要先將問題看過。你可以找出每一個答項當中的動詞嗎？這四個動詞分別是：「吃」、「飛行」、「殺死」以及「看」。

　　在你找到每個答項中的動詞後，利用各個動詞造一個簡單的問句。反問自己：這篇短文是在談論：

how the dodo ate?
多多鳥如何飲食？（不，文章中並未提到這點。）

how the dodo flew?
多多鳥如何飛行？（不，文中沒有提到這點。）

how the dodo killed sailors?
多多鳥如何殺死水手？（同樣地，這點也沒有提到。答案不可能是這個。）

how the dodo looked?
多多鳥長相如何？（是的，看看文中所有描述這種鳥類之外貌的文字，這些字詞很多：「短的」、「肥的」、「黃色的」、「黑色的」、「圓的」等。這篇短文談論到許多關於多多鳥的長相，因此D必定是正確的答案。）

・　Never say die.
　　（永不放棄。）

Text 2 Announcer

播報員

　　(Sports Announcer) And the race is about to begin! Three, two, one! And the racers have begun the race! It looks like the runner from India is running the fastest; he is way out in front. After him is the runner from England, he's running not as fast, but he looks very steady. And the slowest racer is the man from France; right now he's in last place. Can he catch up? But wait! It looks like the fastest man is starting to slow down! Yes, the man from India is falling back, he's not so fast anymore. The steady man from England has taken the lead. He is now closest to the finish line! Yes the runner from England is certainly the faster runner. And he's about to win...Yes! The runner from England has finished the race in first place. And the second place finisher is the runner from India. What an amazing race!

（運動播報員）比賽即將開始了！三、二、一！選手們的競賽開始了。看起來來自印度的選手跑得最快，他遙遙領先。在他後面的是來自英格蘭的選手，他跑得沒那麼快但看起來相當穩定。跑得最慢的選手是來自法國的男士，目前他位居最後。他能夠趕上嗎？等等，看來跑得最快的選手正開始慢下來了。是的，來自印度的選手落後了，他不再那麼快了。來自英格蘭的穩健選手已取得領先，他現在相當接近終點線。沒錯，英格蘭的選手果然是較快的跑者，而他即將要贏了……是的，英格蘭的選手已經奪得比賽的第一名。拿到第二名的是印度的選手。多精采的比賽啊！

 Question and Test Tip Section

D ❶ Which statement best describes the racers at the start of the race?
哪句話最適合形容比賽剛開始時的選手？

A. The slowest runner is from France and the fastest runner is from England.
最慢的選手來自法國，最快的選手來自英格蘭。

B. The fastest runner is from India and the slowest runner is from England.
最快的選手來是印度，最慢的選手來自英格蘭。

C. The slowest runner is from India and the fastest runner is from France.
最慢的選手來自印度，最快的選手來自法國。

D. The fastest runner is from India and the slowest runner is from France.

最快的選手來自印度，最慢的選手來自法國。

解答分析

這個問題是測試你對於副詞fast和slow的最高級形式了解多少。當est附加在像是slow這樣的副詞後面就形成了最高級形式，因此我們就有了slowest這個字代表「最慢」。你必須小心不要將它與其他的副詞形式混淆了，比如slower只代表了「相對程度上較慢」而已。

範例

看看這些使用了slow，big，和tall等副詞的比較級和最高級形式的例子：

A car is slower than an airplane, but a horse is the slowest.

車子比飛機慢，但馬是最慢的。

A dog is bigger than a cat, but a horse is the biggest.

狗比貓大，但馬是最大的。

A chair is taller than a shoe, but a horse is the tallest.

椅子比鞋子高，但馬是最高的。

A ❷ **Which statement best describes the racers at the end of the race?**
哪句話最適合形容比賽結束時的選手？

A. The English runner is faster than the French runner and the Indian runner.
英格蘭選手比法國及印度選手快。

B. The French runner is faster than the Indian runner but slower than the English runner.
法國選手比印度選手快，但比英國選手慢。

C. The Indian runner is slower than the French runner but faster than the English runner.
印度選手比法國選手慢，但比英國選手快。

D. The French and Indian runners are both faster than the English runner.
法國和印度選手都比英國選手快。

- Idleness is the key of beggary.
  （懶惰是貧窮的主要因素。）

Text 3 Harvard ▪ ▪ ▪ ▪ ▪ ▪ ▪ ▪ ▪

哈佛

Harvard University is America's oldest university and one of the most respected. The university was founded in 1636 only a few miles away from the busy colonial city of Boston. The land and books used to start the college were given by a local minister, named John Harvard. To this day the school still carries his name.

哈佛大學是美國最古老,同時也是最有名望的一所大學。這所大學在1636年初建時,距離繁忙的波士頓殖民市區只有幾哩遠。開創大學時所需的土地及書籍,是由一位當地名叫約翰哈佛的官員所貢獻的。直到今天,這所大學仍然沿用這個名字。

When it first began, Harvard was a very small school with only one classroom and one teacher. Only the sons of local political and religious leaders were allowed to attend. But as time passed, the school opened its doors to many more. By 1879, Harvard had begun offering classes to women. Now more than 350 years after its start, Harvard educates men and women from countries all over the world.

初建時，哈佛還是個相當小的學校，只有一個教室和一位教師。並且只有當地政治和宗教領袖的子孫可以被允許就讀。但隨著時間流逝，這所大學也敞開了它的門扉。1879年時，哈佛開始為女性開設課程。如今，在創建之始的三百五十年後，哈佛大學讓來自世界各地的男性及女性在此受教。

 Question and Test Tip Section

<u>C</u> ❶ **Why was the name 'Harvard' chosen for this university?**
為何這所大學要取名為「哈佛」？

A. Because John Harvard was the first student at this school.
因為約翰哈佛是學校的第一個學生。

B. Because John Harvard was the first teacher at this school.
因為約翰哈佛是學校的第一位教師。

Chapter ❸

C. Because John Harvard gave books and land to the school.

因為約翰哈佛提供了書籍和土地給學校。

D. Because John Harvard first let women attend the school.

因為約翰哈佛率先讓女性上學。

解答分析

你看到這個問題的關鍵字了嗎？它們是「為什麼」、「名字」以及「選擇」。（記住，整篇文章以及所有的問題都跟「哈佛大學」有關，因此這兩個單字不會是關鍵字。）

範例

你認識chose這個字嗎？它是動詞choose的過去式，意指「從幾個選項當中挑出某事物」。

The girl saw many colorful dresses, but the pink one was chosen because it was her favorite.

女孩看見許多各式色彩的洋裝，但她選了粉紅色那一件，因為那是她最喜歡的。

讓我們看看其中幾個選項。選項A和B談到「第一個學生」和「第一位教師」，但這篇文章講述的是「第一個學生」和「第一位教師」嗎？不是！因此我們得知A和B都是錯誤的答案。現在你有比較高的機率選到正確的答案了，記住，有時候刪除錯誤的答案，比尋找正確的答案要來得容易。

A ❷ What has changed about Harvard University since it first began?

從初建至今，哈佛大學有什麼改變？

A. It is now open to more people from many countries.

它如今開放給更多來自許多國家的人。

B. Now it is much smaller than when it first began.

它如今比初建時要小多了。

C. It is now only open to people from Boston.

它如今只開放給波士頓的人。

D. Now only people related to politicians can attend.

如今只有與政治家相關的人才能就讀。

解答分析

這個問題比較困難。你必須了解整篇文章的主旨才能正確地回答。如果你現在不知道答案，試著再聽一次這篇文章。不要忘記刪除那些不可能的答案。祝你好運！

Chapter **3**

Text 4 Desk+Book ▪ ▪ ▪ ▪ ▪ ▪ ▪ ▪

書桌與書本

One day Lisa's friend came over to Lisa's house. Her friend, Ruby, wanted to borrow a comic book from Lisa. But Lisa couldn't find the book.

有一天，麗莎的朋友到她家找她。她的朋友露比想要跟她借一本漫畫書。但是麗莎找不到那本書。

"I thought that the book was on top of the desk, but I don't see it," said Lisa.

「我想那本書是放在書桌頂端，但是我看不到它。」麗莎說。

"Maybe the book fell. Did you look under the desk?" asked Ruby.

「也許書本掉下來了。你看過書桌下面了嗎？」露比問。

Then Lisa looked under the desk, but the book was not there.

於是麗莎看看桌下，但書本不在那兒。

"This is very strange," said Lisa and she started looking inside the desk. She looked inside the desk at all of the books and papers, but she did not see the comic book.

「這太奇怪了。」麗莎說，然後她開始在書桌裡頭翻找，她看了抽屜裡所有的書籍和紙張，就是沒有看到那本漫畫書。

"Wait! Maybe the comic book fell behind the desk," said Ruby.

「等等，也許漫畫書掉到書桌後面去了。」露比說。

"That's right, maybe it did," said Lisa and after looking there for less than one minute she said, "I found it!"

「沒錯，搞不好是這樣。」麗莎說。在那裡摸索了不到一分鐘後她說：「我找到了！」

"Wow! That's great. Thank you so much, Lisa," said Ruby as she took the book and went home.

「哇！太好了！真謝謝你，麗莎。」 露比說著，然後帶著書回家了。

 Question and Test Tip Section

A ❶ **Why did Ruby go to Lisa's house?**
為何露比要到麗莎家去？

A. Because she wanted to borrow a comic book.
因為她想要借一本漫畫書。

B. Because she wanted to look at her desk.
因為她想要看看她的書桌。

C. Because she wanted to help Lisa work.
因為她想幫麗莎工作。

D. Because she wanted to give Lisa a book.
因為她想要給麗莎一本書。

> **解答分析**
>
> 這個問題用why問，詢問露比到麗莎家的原因。

B ❷ Where did they finally find the comic book?
她們最後在哪裡找到漫畫書？

A. The comic book was on the desk.
漫畫書在書桌上。

B. The comic book was behind the desk.
漫畫書在書桌後面。

C. The comic book was under the desk.
漫畫書在書桌下面。

D. The comic book was inside the desk.
漫畫書在書桌裡頭。

> **解答分析**
>
> 這是一個測試你對介系詞了解程度的問題。答案可能不容易得到，因為文中使用了there這個代名詞。記住，代名詞是用來取代名詞的字。把加粗的句子再讀一遍，然後找出there所代替的地點。

Chapter ❸

Text 5 Chair-speech ▪ ▫ ▪ ▫ ▪ ▫ ▪ ▫ ▫

主席演講

Good afternoon workers of the EZ-Sit Chair Company, I am your boss Mr. Harmond. Today is a very special day for our company and all of its employees. During the last six months, our company increased production by nearly ten percent; we made over 2,500 more chairs than we did in the same amount of time last year. Because of this, our company was able to earn more money, and the value of our company's stock also increased.

各位舒適座椅公司的員工們，大家午安。我是你們的老闆，哈爾孟德。今天對於我們公司以及所有員工而言是個特別的日子，在過去六個月當中，公司的生產量增加了將近百分之十，比去年同時期的座椅產量多了超過兩千五百張。由於這點，我們的公司將會有更多盈利，而公司的股值也會提高。

I would like to announce that to celebrate these important accomplishments we will be having a company event this Saturday. I have purchased tickets for all of you and your families to attend the Red Sox baseball game. The game begins at 7 pm, at the baseball stadium on Fenway Street. Please meet in the parking lot section 3-B by 6:30 pm where I will be giving out the tickets.

我在此宣布,為了慶祝這些重要的成果,本週六我們將舉辦一項公司活動。我已經為各位以及各位的家屬購買了Red Sox籃球賽的入場票,比賽從下午七點開始,地點在芬威街的籃球場。請在六點半時到停車場3-B區集合,到時我會把票發給各位。

In conclusion, I would just like to express my personal thanks and appreciation for all of the hard work that you have put into the EZ-Sit Chair Company. Without your help, this company could not be as strong, or successful, as it is today. Thanks again, and I'll see you on Saturday.

最後,我想要向所有對舒適座椅公司付出的努力表達我個人的感激之情。沒有你們的幫助,公司無法像今日這般茁壯及成功。再次謝謝各位,星期六見!

Question and Test Tip Section

<u>C</u> ❶ **Who was the person that read this statement?**
朗誦這篇講稿的是誰？

A. a baseball player
一個籃球選手

B. the person who bought a chair
買了一張椅子的人

C. the boss of the chair company
座椅公司的老闆

D. a worker in the chair company
座椅公司的一位員工

解答分析

這個問題的答案並沒有被直接陳述出來。你必須把第一句話聽幾遍，直到你了解代名詞「我」所代表的名詞是誰。

A ❷ Why did the person make this statement?
何以此人要發表這篇演說？

A. Because the company has been successful and has earned more money.

因為公司一直相當成功，賺了更多錢。

B. Because the company needs to earn more money so the employees must all work harder.

因為公司必須賺進更多錢，因此員工必須更加努力工作。

C. Because too many employees have been going to baseball games instead of going to work.

因為太多員工跑去看籃球賽而不努力工作。

D. Because the employees can go to baseball games instead of going on vacation.

因為員工可以去看籃球賽卻不能休假。

解答分析

這個問題測試你對於這篇短文的了解程度。演講者是否說過他很感激呢？或者他很生氣？演講者想要傳達的主要思想是什麼呢？

<u>D</u> ❸ **When will the employees be meeting in the baseball stadium's parking lot?**
員工們何時要在籃球場的停車場集合？

A. They will meet at 7:00 pm on Saturday evening.
他們會在星期六傍晚七點集合。

B. They will be meeting after the game on Saturday.
他們會在星期六比賽結束後集合。

C. They will all go together to the parking lot after work.
他們全部會在下班後到停車場集合。

D. They will be meeting at 6:30 pm on Saturday.
他們會在星期六下午六點半集合。

- Time and tide wait for no man.
  （歲月不饒人，時光不待人。）

Text 6 Pisa ■ ■ ■ ■ ■ ■ ■ ■ ■ ■ ■

比薩斜塔

The Leaning Tower of Pisa is one of the most famous buildings in the world. It is a round tower made of white stone and stands over fifty meters tall. But what most people know about the tower is that it does not stand straight, it leans nearly six degrees to one side.

比薩斜塔是世界上最有名的建築之一。它是一座由白色石頭建成的圓塔，高度超過五十公尺。但這座塔最為人所熟知的是：它並非直立的，塔的其中一邊傾斜了將近六十度。

Construction of the tower began in the 1100's. After they had completed only three stories, the builders realized that one side of the building was slowly sinking into the ground. So they stopped building to look for a solution. They decided to make the short side taller by adding more stones. But this did not help. The extra stones caused the short side to be heavier, which made it sink into the ground even faster!

這座塔從十二世紀開始建造。在只有完成三層樓的時候，建築師發現這棟建築的一側輕微地傾向地面；因此他們停止建造並尋求解決之道。他們決定藉由添加更多的石頭將較矮的一側撐高。但這個方法沒有奏效。多餘的石頭使得低矮的那一側變得更重，也使它加快了傾向地面的速度。

The eight story tower was completed by the 1300's. Over the years, people have tried several times to make the leaning tower stand up straight. In 1990 the tower was closed and builders tried once again to straighten the tower, this time with more success. After nearly ten years of slow digging, they managed to straighten the tower by about 0.2 meters. Today, it still stands in Italy as one of the most recognized buildings in the world.

這棟八層的塔於十四世紀時完成。多年來，人們多次嘗試要將這棟傾斜的塔扶正。斜塔在1990年時關閉，建築師們又再次嘗試將塔豎直，這一次獲得了較大的成功。在將近十年的緩慢挖鑿下，他們成功地將斜塔扶正約0.2公尺。如今，這座全世界最著名的建築之一仍然屹立於義大利。

Question and Test Tip Section

<u>B</u> ❶ **Why is the Leaning Tower of Pisa a famous building?**
比薩斜塔何以是有名的建築？

A. Because it was built so long ago using very old stones.

因為它在很久以前以古老的石塊建造而成。

B. Because it doesn't stand straight, but leans to one side.

因為它不是直立的，而是傾向一邊。

C. Because it was mostly completed in the 1300's in Italy.

因為它大部分完成於十四世紀時的義大利。

D. Because it is one of the tallest buildings in the world.

因為它是世界上最高的建築之一。

Chapter ❸

解答分析

你找到這個問題的關鍵字了嗎？它們是「為什麼」以及「有名的」。（記得比薩斜塔是本篇的主題。）你知道famous 這個形容詞嗎？它表示某人或某事物是廣為大眾所知悉的。

<u>C</u> ❷ **How did builders in the 1100's attempt to straighten the tower?**
十二世紀的建築師嘗試以何種方式使斜塔直立？

A. They dug a hole around the bottom of the tower.

他們在塔底的周圍挖一個洞。

B. They added more stones to the tall side of the tower.

他們在斜塔較高的那一側添加更多石頭。

C. They added more stones to the short side of the tower.

他們在斜塔較矮的那一側添加更多石頭。

D. They finished all eight stories before it began to lean.

他們在斜塔開始傾斜之前完成了所有的八層。

解答分析

你找到這個問題的關鍵字了嗎？它們是「如何」、「建築師」、「十二世紀」、「嘗試」、「使直立」以及「塔」。

你認識builder這個字嗎？builder這個字的來源是動詞build，build是指建築或組成。builder則是指從事建築的人。在英文裡，"er"結尾的字通常是指從事這個動作的人。

範例

teach/teacher: A teacher is a person who teaches.

老師是指施教的人。

drive/driver: A driver is a person who drives.

司機是指開車的人。

play/player: A player is a person who plays.

選手是指進行運 的人。

swim/swimmer: A swimmer is a person who swims.

泳者是指游泳的人。

learn/learner: A learner is a person who learns.

學習者是指學習的人。

解答分析

要注意，這篇文章談論到兩個使斜塔直立的做法。其中一個發生在十二世紀，另一個則始於1990年代。這個問題只問到十二世紀那個做法，不要被弄錯了。

Chapter 3

• To save time is to lengthen life.
（節約時間就是延長生命。）

B ❸ **Which of the following statements about the Leaning Tower of Pisa is true?**
下列哪個有關比薩斜塔的敘述是正確的？

A. Although the tower is not straight, builders have never attempted to make it straighter.

雖然此塔不是直立的，但建築師從未嘗試將它扶正。

B. Because the tower is not straight, builders have tried several times to make it straighter.

由於此塔不正，建築師多次嘗試使它變得較直。

C. The tower stood straight for a long time, but has only recently begun to lean to one side.

這座塔直立了很長一段時間，是最近才開始傾斜的。

D. In the past 600 years, the tower has slowly become straighter and straighter.

過去六百年來，這座塔慢慢地變得愈來愈直了。

解答分析

許多英文考試會問到：「下列哪個敘述是真實的？」。大致說來，只有一個答項會是正確的，其餘的則是錯誤的。然而，你必須小心地閱讀每一個選項，因為有些選項可能半真半假。例如選項A：「雖然此塔不是直立的，但建築師從未嘗試將它扶正。」

這個句子被一個逗點分成了兩個部分，第一個部分是對的，但第二個部分卻是錯的。因此，在你做決定前，你必須讀完各個選項句子的每一個部分。

Text 7 Trash ■ ■ ■ ■ ■ ■ ■ ■ ■ ■ ■

垃圾

Not too long ago many places in America had a big problem with garbage. What was the problem? There was too much garbage! But now, many cities and states have taken some big steps towards improving this serious problem. Let's take a look and see what people are doing to help improve the situation.

不久前，美國的許多地方擁有垃圾方面的大麻煩。什麼麻煩呢？垃圾太多了！但如今，許多城市和州已經採取了一些改善這個大問題的強力措施了。讓我們看看人們對於改善這個情況做了什麼事情。

Plastic bags have long been used all over the world to carry things home from the store. Before, if you'd gone to the store to buy, maybe, some bread and water, then the store would have given you a free plastic bag. You would then have used this bag to carry your bread and water home, and then thrown it away. And this lead to a big problem: there were too many plastic bags thrown away!

塑膠袋長久以來在全世界各地被使用，人們用它從商店提東西回家。以前，如果你到商店去買麵包和水，店家可能會提供免費的塑膠袋給你。然後你提著裝有麵包和水的塑膠袋回家之後就把它丟了。而這導致了一個問題：有太多的塑膠袋被丟棄。

Slowly, city leaders started to realize that too many plastic bags were making the garbage problem worse. Then some cities decided to make people pay a little money for each plastic bag they used. Now, people are all using fewer plastic bags. And, because they cost us money, we've stopped throwing them into the garbage!

漸漸地，市府領導人開始意識到太多的塑膠袋將使得垃圾問題更加嚴重。於是，有些城市決定讓人民為他們所使用的每一個塑膠袋付一點費用。如今，人們使用的塑膠袋數量變少了。而且由於塑膠袋需要花錢買，我們也不再將塑膠袋丟入垃圾當中。

Of course, the world still has a problem with garbage. But some American cities have recently made a big accomplishment: they've got people to use and throw away fewer plastic bags. This means less garbage to throw away, and less garbage for the world!

當然，這個世界仍然面臨垃圾問題。但有些美國城市最近有了很大的進展：它們促使人民使用及丟棄更少的塑膠袋。這意味著被丟掉的塑膠袋變少了，世界上的垃圾也變少了。

 Question and Test Tip Section

C ❶ **What have some American cities recently accomplished?**
某些美國城市最近達成了什麼事情？

A. They've allowed people to make more garbage.
它們已允許人民製造更多垃圾。

B. They've made plastic bags illegal.
它們視塑膠袋為不合法之物。

C. They've made people use and throw away fewer plastic bags.

使人民減少使用和丟棄塑膠袋。

D. They've solved the problem of having too much garbage.

它們已解決垃圾太多的問題。

解答分析

"accomplish"這個字表示完善地做完某事,它通常代表將某事做得很好。

範例

The student worked very hard and accomplished her goal of learning Japanese.

這個學生非常用功,且達到她學習日文的目標。

- **Every minute counts.**

（分秒必爭。）

<u>B</u> ❷ What did the government decide to do?
政府決定怎麼做？

A. They decided never to use plastic bags.

他們決定永不使用塑膠袋。

B. They decided to make people pay for plastic bags.

他們決定讓人民付費使用塑膠袋。

C. They decided to give everyone plastic bags.

他們決定發放塑膠袋給每個人。

D. They decided that plastic bags are not a problem.

他們決定塑膠袋將不是問題所在。

解答分析

你能找到第二題的關鍵字嗎？這些字是「什麼」、「政府」和「決定」。現在，當你聆聽文章時，你得注意何時聽到「決定」這個字，因為它是這個問題的動詞。如果有好幾個關鍵字，那麼你應該將焦點放在動詞上面；第一題是「完成」，而這題是「決定」。這文章中含有「決定」這個字的句子將是本題的答案。

Chapter **3**

Part ❷ Dialogue Question 對話試題

There are 9 dialogues in this section, each dialogue has 1~2 questions. Please listen to the CD and choose the right answers, every dialogue will be read twice.

本單元包括九個對話題，每個題目會有一到二個問題。請聽CD作答，選出正確答案，每題會唸二遍。

Dialogue 1 Haircut ▪ ▪ ▪ ▪ ▪ ▪ ▪ ▪

剪頭髮

Man	Hello. Can I help you? 哈囉，需要為您效勞嗎？

Woman	Yes, I'd like a wash and trim. 是的，我想要洗頭、修一下頭髮。

Man	Would you like it cut very short? 你想要剪得很短嗎？

Woman	Well, I really want to cut just a little bit off. 嗯，我只想要剪掉一點點。
Man	Should I cut the hair above your ears? 要剪到耳朵以上嗎？
Woman	No. Just make it shorter in the front and back. 不用，前後各剪短一點就好了。

 Question and Test Tip Section

<u>C</u> **What is this woman doing?**
這個女人在做什麼？

A. She is playing a game.
她在玩遊戲。

B. She is cutting some papers.
她正在剪一些紙張。

Chapter ❸

C. She is getting her hair cut.

她在剪頭髮。

D. She is talking to a doctor.

她在和一位醫生講話。

解答分析

你認識cut（修剪）這個字嗎？它表示：將某物剪短一些，使之更整齊或更好看。

範例

The gardener trimmed all of the plants and trees to make them look better.

園丁修剪了所有的植物及樹木，使它們更好看了。

- **Take time when time comes.**

（機不可失。）

Dialogue 2 Borrow ■ ■ ■ ■ ■ ■ ■ ■

借東西

Mary	Hey, can I borrow your new dictionary? 嘿，我可以跟你借你的新字典嗎？

Jeff	Don't you still have my other dictionary? 我的另一本字典不是還在你那兒嗎？

Mary	I did, but I gave it to my friend and he lost it. 是啊，可是我給了我的朋友，他卻把它搞丟了。

Jeff	You lost my other dictionary? 你搞丟了我的另一本字典？

| Mary | No, my friend lost it. So, can I borrow your new one?
不是我，是我朋友弄丟的。那麼我可以跟你借那本新的嗎？ |

| Jeff | Sorry, but you didn't take care of the other one that I lent to you. So I don't want to lend you my new one.
很抱歉，你沒有好好保管我借給你的另一本。因此我不想再把我的新字典借給你了。 |

 Question and Test Tip Section

B **What does Jeff _not_ want to do?**
傑夫不想做什麼事情？

A. He doesn't want to use Mary's dictionary.
他不想使用瑪莉的字典。

B. He doesn't want to lend Mary his dictionary.
他不想把字典借給瑪莉。

C. He doesn't want to buy a new dictionary.
他不想買新字典。

D. He doesn't want to borrow a dictionary.
他不想跟別人借字典。

解答分析

你必須了解"borrow"和"lend"之間的差別才有辦法正確地回答這個問題。某物的主人可以將此物借(lend)給他人；而其他人則是向主人借(borrow)此物。

範例

This is Alice's car. She can lend her car to Joe. Joe can borrow the car from Alice.
這是愛莉絲的車子。她可以把車子借給喬。喬可以向愛莉絲借車子。

Dialogue 3 Cake ■ ■ ■ ■ ■ ■ ■ ■ ■

蛋糕

Sally	Would you like to try some chocolate cake? 你想要嚐嚐巧克力蛋糕嗎？
Jerry	Sure, I'll try a piece. 傑瑞：好啊，我想要試一片。
Sally	My mother made it for my birthday. 我媽媽為了我的生日做的。
Jerry	Wow! It's very good. But... 哇，很好吃，但是……
Sally	But what? 但是什麼？
Jerry	It's very, very sweet! 太甜了！
Sally	Yes, my mom uses a lot of sugar when she cooks! 是啊，我媽媽做的時候放了很多糖。

Jerry	That's okay. It's still very good. 沒關係，還是很好吃。

Sally	Thanks. I'll tell her that you like it. 謝謝，我會告訴她你很喜歡。

 Question and Test Tip Section

D ❶ Who made the chocolate cake?
誰做了這個巧克力蛋糕？

A. Jerry made the cake.
傑瑞做了這塊蛋糕。

B. Sally made the cake.
莎莉做了這塊蛋糕。

C. Jerry's mother made the cake.
傑瑞的媽媽做了這塊蛋糕。

D. Sally's mother made the cake.
莎莉的媽媽做了這塊蛋糕。

Chapter **3**

解答分析

你找到這個問題裡頭的關鍵字了嗎？這些關鍵字是「誰」、「製作」和「蛋糕」。無疑地，「誰」這個字是個疑問詞，用來詢問哪個人做了某件事；在這個問題中，who和動詞"made"配在一起。當你在聽這個對話時，仔細聽有提到誰做了這個蛋糕（或者"it"）的句子；"it"是個代名詞。你知道"it"在這裡代表的是什麼嗎？這個對話當中，it被使用了五次，代表的是這塊巧克力蛋糕。

<u>D</u> ❷ **What does Jeff think of the chocolate cake?**

傑夫認為這塊巧克力蛋糕怎麼樣？

A. He thinks it's not very sweet and doesn't taste good.

他覺得不是很甜而且不好吃。

B. He thinks it's very sweet and doesn't taste good.

他覺得太甜了不好吃。

C. He thinks it's not very sweet and tastes very good.

他覺得不是很甜但很好吃。

D. He thinks it's very sweet and tastes very good.

他覺得非常甜而且很好吃。

Dialogue 4 Bathroom ■ ■ ■ ■ ■ ■ ■

洗手間

Man	Excuse me, could you tell me where the bathroom is? 不好意思，請告訴我洗手間在哪裡好嗎？
Woman	Yes, the bathroom is on the third floor, across from the camera store. 嗯，洗手間在三樓，照相館的對面。
Man	I see. But...which floor is this? 我知道了。不過……這裡是幾樓呢？
Woman	We are on the fourth floor now. 這裡是四樓。
Man	So I need to go down to the third floor. And... then...? 所以我得下去三樓。然後呢……？

Woman	Go down one floor, and then find the camera store. 往下一層，然後找照相館。

Man	And the bathroom is across from, or next to, the camera store? 然後洗手間就在照相館對面，或者隔壁？

Woman	It's across from the camera store. 是在照相館對面。

Man	Thanks for your help. 謝謝你的幫忙。

Woman	You're welcome. Have a nice day. 不客氣。祝你有愉快的一天。

- Time lost cannot be won again.
  （時光流逝，不可復得。）

- Time past cannot be called back again.
  （時間不能倒流。）

Question and Test Tip Section

A Where is the bathroom?
洗手間在哪裡？

A. The bathroom is on the third floor across from the camera store.

洗手間在三樓的照相館對面。

B. The bathroom is on the third floor next to the camera store.

洗手間在三樓的照相館隔壁。

C. The bathroom is on the fourth floor across from the camera store.

洗手間在四樓的照相館對面。

D. The bathroom is on the fourth floor next to the camera store.

洗手間在四樓的照相館隔壁。

解答分析

這個問題測試你對介系詞的了解。介系詞是英文中很重要的
一部分，因為它們有時候不容易掌握。介系詞通常被使用成
介系詞片語，而且每個介系詞都必定有一個受詞。

Chapter **3**

範例

We watched a movie in the airplane.
我們在飛機上看電影．。

"in the airplane"是個介系詞片語，而"in"是介系詞。

"the airplane"是介系詞"in"的受詞。

現在看看這個例子

I went to see the doctor but he wasn't in.
我去看醫生可是他不在……。

又是"in"這個字，但是這個句子中的in不是介系詞，而是轉化成形容詞（在的）。因為它並非一個片語的一部分而且也沒有受詞。

常使用的介系詞

about 在附近	above 在之上	across 穿越
after 在之後	against 抵著	along 沿著
among 在之中	around 在附近	at 在
before 在之前	behind 在之上	below 在之下
beneath 在之下	beside 在旁邊	between 在之間
beyond 在之上	by 靠著	down 在之下
during 在期間	except 除了以外	for 為了
from 來自	in 在裡面	inside 在裡面
into 進入	like 如同	near 在附近
of 的	off 在外面	on 在上面
out 在外面	outside 外面的	over 在
past 經過	since 自從	through 穿過
to 到	toward 朝向	under 在之下
until 直到	up 向上	upon 在上面
with 連同	within 在裡面	without 沒有

　　了解介系詞的最好方法就是練習使用它們，並且當你在一個句子中聽到介系詞時注意聆聽它們。

Chapter ❸

Dialogue 5 Pronoun ■ ■ ■ ■ ■ ■ ■

代名詞

M Did you hear what Joe said to Mrs. Whitefield?
你聽到喬對懷特菲爾德太太說的話嗎？

W No. What did he say to her?
沒有，他對她說了什麼？

M He said that she was wasting too much water washing her car.
他說她洗車子的時候浪費了太多水了。

W Really? Then what did she say to him?
真的嗎？那她又回他什麼話呢？

M Then she said that he should mind his own business!
她說他應該管好自己的事情就好啦！

W	Wow! That wasn't a nice thing for her to say. 哇！她這樣說真是不太好。

M	No, he felt embarrassed and then he said that he was sorry. 那可不，他覺得很尷尬，然後就說他很抱歉。

Question and Test Tip Section

B Which person was washing their car?
誰洗了車子呢？

A. Joe
喬。

B. Mrs. Whitefield
懷特菲爾德太太。

C. Both Joe and Mrs. Whitefield
喬和懷特菲爾德太太。

D. Neither Joe nor Mrs. Whitefield
喬和懷特菲爾德太太都沒有洗車。

解答分析

這個對話是測試你對於代名詞的理解程度。代名詞是代替一個名詞的字。在這篇對話中，主要的代名詞是"he/his"以及"she/her"。你必須要專注聽第一個句子並且找出"he"和"she"指的是誰。當然，如果只要你記住**he**指的是一個喬這樣的男性而**she**指的是譬如懷特菲爾德太太這樣的女性，那就容易多了。

- He who works before dawn will soon be his own master. （黎明前早起工作的人，將做自己的主人。）

- An hour in the morning is worth two in the evening. （一日之計在於晨。）

Dialogue 6 CopTV

警匪片

James	Wow! That car is going so fast! 哇，那部車子開太快了。
Joyce	Yeah, but that police car is right behind it! 是啊，不過那部警車就在它後面。
James	Oh no! He almost crashed into that big tree. 喔，不好！他差點撞上那棵大樹。
Joyce	It looks like the police car is slowing down... 看起來那輛警車慢下來了……
James	I don't think the police car is fast enough. 我覺得那輛警車開得不夠快。

Chapter **3**

Joyce	Right, it looks like the bad guy has already gotten away. 沒錯，看來那個壞胚子已經逃掉了。
James	Do you want to keep watching this? 你要繼續看這個嗎？
Joyce	No, the policeman gave up. What do you want to watch instead? 不了，那個警察放棄了。那你想看什麼呢？
James	Can we watch the news? 看新聞好不好？
Joyce	Sure, that's fine with me. 好啊，我贊成。

Question and Test Tip Section

B ❶ Where did James and Joyce see the police car?
詹姆斯和喬依斯在哪裡看警車？

A. near their home
他們家附近。

B. on a television show

在一個電視節目上。

C. next to a newspaper

報社隔壁。

D. all of the above

以上皆是。

A ❷ Why could the police car not catch the other car?

為什麼警車沒有追上另一輛車子？

A. Because the police car could not drive fast enough.

因為警車開得不夠快。

B. Because the police car was driving fast and crashed into a tree.

因為警察開得太快以致於撞上了一棵樹木。

C. Because the other car was always right behind the police car.

因為另一輛車子總是跟在警車後面。

D. Because the other car was not driving as fast as the police car.

因為另一輛車子開得不像警車那麼快。

Dialogue 7 Directions ■ ■ ■ ■ ■ ■ ■

引導

| Jeff | Hello, is this Linda?
哈囉，是琳達嗎？ |

| Linda | Yes, hi Jeff, how can I help you?
是啊，嗨，傑夫，什麼事情嗎？ |

| Jeff | Well, I think I might be lost. Can you give me some directions?
是這樣的，我想我大概迷路了。你能給我一點指引嗎？ |

| Linda | Yes, of course. What do you need to know?
當然好啊。你想要知道什麼？ |

| Jeff | Should I turn left or right on Main Street?
我應該在中央大道上左轉還是右轉呢？ |

Linda	You should turn left on Main Street, and then go straight until you reach the stop sign. 你應該在中央大道上左轉，然後往前走一直到紅綠燈。

Jeff	Okay. What should I do when I reach the next stop sign? 好的。當我到達下一個紅綠燈時要怎麼走呢？

Linda	Turn right at the next stop sign and then drive straight for about three miles. 在下一個紅綠燈右轉，然後往前開大約三哩。

Jeff	Okay. I'll turn left and then keep going straight. 沒問題。我會左轉然後繼續往前走。

Linda	Now look for the high school on the left side, right after the park. 現在往左手邊找一座中學，就在過了公園以後。

Chapter **3**

| Jeff | Okay, I see the park. And there is the high school. Now what should I do?
好的，我看到公園了，還有一座中學在那裡。現在我要怎麼走？ |

| Linda | Turn onto the street by the high school and find a place to park.
轉到中學旁邊那條街道，然後找個停車位。 |

| Jeff | And after I've parked can I walk to your house?
我停好車以後可以用走的到你家嗎？ |

| Linda | Yes, my house is right behind the high school.
沒錯，我家就在那所中學後面。 |

| Jeff | Thank you!
謝啦！ |

| Linda | You're welcome. See you soon!
不客氣。待會兒見！ |

Question and Test Tip Section

<u>C</u> ❶ What is the man doing?
這個男人在做什麼？

A. The man is driving a car and listening to the radio.

這個男人正在一面開車一面聽收音機。

B. The man is walking on the street and eating.

這個男人在街上邊走路邊吃東西。

C. The man is driving a car and talking to the woman.

這個男人正一面開車一面跟一個女人講話。

D. The man is walking on the street and looking for the park.

這個男人正在街上走著並且尋找一座公園。

解答分析

這些選項也都包含了兩個子句。記得在選擇答案前先確定兩個句子都是正確的。

你能夠從對話中分辨出這個男人是在走路或者開車嗎？這有點困難，因為「開車」和「走路」這兩個字在對話中都沒有出現。但有幾個提示的字可以幫助你下決定。例如，「尋找停車場」這個片語可以幫助你了解這個男人是在開車並非在走路。

A ❷ Which word could replace the word 'right' in the sentence 'My house is right behind the school'?

哪個字可以代替'My house is right behind the school'這個句子中的"right"這個字？

A. directly

　　直接地；就……

B. wrong

　　錯誤的

C. left

　　左邊

D. correct

　　正確地

解答分析

"Right"這個字有許多不同的意思。這裡有一些right最常用的意思以及其例句。

範例

1. Right and Left (directional).
   左邊和右邊（指方向）。

Example: The pen is in my right hand and the pencil is in my left hand.

例句 ： 鋼筆在我的右手邊而鉛筆在我左手邊。

2. Right and Wrong (correct and incorrect).
對和錯（正確和不正確）。

Example: The answer the girl gave is right, but the boy's answer is wrong.

例句 ： 這女孩給的答案是對的，但這男孩給的答案是錯誤的。

3. Right (meaning 'directly').
就是／就在（表示直接地）。

Example: Be careful, the little boy is standing right behind you. Or: We can go see the movie right after I make this phone call.

例句 ： 小心，小男孩就站在你後面。／我打完這通電話後我們就可以直接去看電影了。

三個 "right" 得不同含義

The right answer is right in front of the book on the right of the table.
正確的答案就在桌子右邊的書本前面。

Dialogue 8 Reservations ■ ■ ■ ■ ■ ■

訂位

M Good afternoon. This is Louigi's Fine Dining. How may I help you?
午安。這裡是「路基精緻餐廳」，需要我效勞嗎？

W Yes, could you please tell me a little about your menu?
是的，可以請你提供一些關於你們菜單的資訊嗎？

M Certainly. We offer a selection of Italian dishes, homemade noodles, freshly baked breads and Italian ice cream.
當然。我們供應整套義大利菜，有家鄉麵、新鮮的烤麵包和義大利冰淇淋。

W I see, that sounds very good. Are reservations required?
我了解的，聽起來很棒。需要訂位嗎？

M We do not require reservations, but they are recommended for the weekends.

不用，但如果是週末我們建議您這樣做。

W Well then, I'd like to make reservations for this Saturday evening.

那麼，我想要訂這個週六傍晚的席位。

M For what time?

幾點鐘呢？

W How about 7 o'clock?

七點可以嗎？

M 7 o'clock is fine. And how many people will be dining?

七點沒問題。會有幾個人用餐呢？

W There will be four of us.

我們會有四個人。

Chapter **3**

M	And your name, please? 請告訴我你的名字好嗎？

W	My name is Miss Stevenson. 我是史蒂芬森小姐。

M	Thank you Miss Stevenson. We will see you on Saturday at 7 o'clock. 謝謝你，史蒂芬森小姐。星期六七點見！

W	Thank you. Good bye. 謝謝。再見。

 Question and Test Tip Section

D ❶ **Why does the woman ask her first question?**
這位女士問的第一個問題目的為何？

A. Because she wants to know where the restaurant is located.
她想知道餐廳的地點在哪裡。

B. Because she wants to know the name of the restaurant.

她想知道餐廳的名字。

C. Because she wants to know how large the restaurant is.

她想知道餐廳有多大。

D. Because she wants to know what kind of food the restaurant has.

她想知道這家餐廳提供哪些種類的食物。

解答分析

又來了，注意看這四個選項有多麼相似。你應該將焦點放在不同的疑問詞以及疑問片語上面：「哪裡」、「什麼名字」、「多大」以及「什麼種類」。記住，將答項的句子成分改成新的、簡單些的問題，通常會有助益。你可以練習將答句改成問句：

Q: Does the woman's first question ask:
這個女人的第一個問題是問：

A: where the restaurant is?
餐廳在哪裡？

B: what the name of the restaurant is?
餐廳的名字？

C: how large the restaurant is?
餐廳有多大？

D: what kind of food the restaurant has?
餐廳提供哪些食物？

<u>B</u> ❷ **Does this restaurant require reservations?**
這家餐廳需要訂位嗎？

A. The restaurant requires reservations for very large groups of people.
假如是群組聚會就要訂位。

B. The restaurant does not require reservations, but they are recommended for weekends.
這家餐廳無須訂位，但週末最好事先訂位。

C. The restaurant requires reservations for every day of the week.
這家餐廳一星期中的每一天都需要訂位。

D. The restaurant recommends reservations for weekdays, but they are not required for weekends.
這家餐廳建議平日要訂位，但週末則不用。

解答分析

這個問題測試你對於這兩組單字的了解程度。分別是 weekday／weekend以及require／recommend。

範例一

weekdays 是指一個禮拜當中的星期一到星期五。

例： He goes to work on the weekdays from 9 am until 6 pm.

他平日從早上九點上班到下午六點。

weekend 是指一個禮拜中的最後兩天，也就是星期六和星期天。

例： Because he spends every weekday in the city, he likes to go to the mountains on the weekends.

由於他平時每天都待在都市裡，週末時他喜歡到山上走走。

範例二

用"required"形容某事是表示它是必要的、或者必須要做。

例： Our school requires that students wear the school uniform. Students that do not wear the uniform will not be allowed to come to school.

我們學校要求每個學生一定要穿校服。沒有穿校服的學生不准到學校來。

Chapter ❸

範例三

用"recommended"敘述某事是指此事乃是建議、或者它應該被做比較好。

例：The teacher recommends that we read this book. We are not required to read the book, but the teacher suggests that we read it.
老師建議我們讀這本書。我們並非被要求非得讀這本書不可，但是老師建議我們讀它。

- Fear not the future; weep not for the past.
  （不要畏懼未來，也不要為過去而哭泣。）

- He who could foresee affairs three days in advance would be rich for thousands of years.
  （能預知三日後事物的人，能富有千年。）

- It's not enough to run, one must start in time.
  （光會跑不夠，還得及時開跑。）

- Live only for today, and you ruin tomorrow.
  （若只為今日而活，你將毀掉明天。）

Dialogue 9 Coffee

咖啡

Cashier	Hello. Can I help you? 哈囉，需要我幫忙嗎？
Customer	Yes, I'd like a large latte, one small coffee, and a medium iced tea. 是的，我想要一杯大杯的拿鐵、一杯小杯的咖啡、和一杯中杯的冰紅茶。
Cashier	Would you like sugar in the iced tea? 冰紅茶要加糖嗎？
Customer	No. But can you add a little lemon? 不要。但是可以加一點檸檬嗎？

Chapter **3**

Cashier	No problem. Would you like cream in the coffee? 沒問題。咖啡要加一點奶精嗎？

Customer	Yes please, but none in the latte. 好，不過拿鐵不用加。

Cashier	Very well. And will you be needing anything else today? 好的。你還需要其他任何東西嗎？

Customer	No thank you. That is all. 不用了，謝謝。這樣就好。

Cashier	Will this be for here or to go? 要這裡用還是外帶？

Customer	To go, please. What is the total of all of this? 我要帶走，謝謝。總共多少錢？

Cashier	That will be $5.25. 這樣是五塊二十五毛錢。

Question and Test Tip Section

<u>B</u> ❶ **Where did this conversation take place?**
這個對話是在哪裡發生的？

A. In a police station.
在一個警察局裡頭。

B. In a coffee shop.
在一家咖啡館。

C. In a farmhouse.
在一座農場裡。

D. In a flower store.
在一家花店裡頭。

解答分析

注意這個問題，"take"這個字有超過二十種不同的意思。
你知道"take place"的意思嗎？它的意思是「發生」或「舉行」。

範例

The basketball game will take place in the high school.
籃球賽將在這所中學舉行。

Chapter ❸

這個問題可以被改寫成"Where did this conversation happen (or occur)? "

<u>D</u> ❷ **In the customer's last sentence, what does the phrase 'To go, please' mean?**
在顧客所說的最後一句話當中，"to go, please"代表什麼意思？

A. He would like to hurry up and go and sit down.
他想要快點離開然後坐下。

B. He would like the other man to go away.
他希望另一個人離開。

C. He would like to take the other man to go somewhere.
他想要帶另一個人到某地方去。

D. He would like to take his drinks out of the store.
他要帶著他的飲料離開這家咖啡店。

Part **3** Picture Question 圖畫試題

This section include 7 pictures, each picture has 1~2 questions, please look at the pictures, listen to the CD, and choose the best answer for each question, every question and options will be read twice.
本單元包括七張圖，每張圖有一到二個題目，請看圖聽Ｃ
Ｄ，並選出最正確的答案，每題的題目及選項均各唸二遍。

Pictur 1 Bookstore

書店

　　圖片上有三個女孩在一家書店裡。莎莉正握著一本
書，而麗莎和瑪莉則沒有拿書。麗莎有著很長的頭髮，
莎莉是中長髮，而瑪莉則是短髮。

Question and Test Tip Section

<u>C</u> ❶ **Which description of the three girls is correct?**
對這三個女孩的描述哪個是正確的？

A. All the girls are carrying a book.
所有的女孩都拿著一本書。

B. Most of the girls are carrying a book.
大部分的女孩都拿著一本書。

C. One girl is carrying a book.
其中一個女孩拿著一本書。

D. None of the girls are carrying books.
沒有女孩拿著書本。

解答分析

現在看看第一題的所有選項。你可以看出來它們的型態上大致相同嗎？只有每個選項的第一個字有所改變而已。看看這四個單字：「所有」、「大部分」、「一個」和「沒有」。每一個字都是代表著告訴我們有多少女孩拿著書本的形容詞。現在回到圖片上，答案或許就更明顯了。

看看第一題。你知道"description"這個字的意思嗎？它表示向你描述某事物是什麼、正在做什麼或者長得怎麼樣。

> **範例**
>
> The description of his dog says that it is big, has a brown body, and black and white ears.
>
> 對於他的狗的描述顯示它很大、有著棕色的身體、以及白色和黑色的耳朵。

<u>D</u> ❷ **Which of the three girls has the longest hair?**

三個女孩之中哪一個的頭髮最長？

A. They all have long hair.

她們都是長頭髮。

B. Sally has the longest hair.

莎莉頭髮最長。

C. Mary has the longest hair.

瑪莉頭髮最長。

D. Lisa has the longest hair.

麗莎頭髮最長。

Chapter **3**

• A fool's bolt may sometimes hit the mark.

（愚者千慮，必有一得。）

Pictur 2 Pie Chart ■ ■ ■ ■ ■ ■ ■ ■ ■ ■

圓形圖

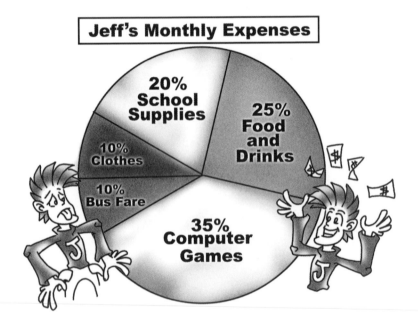

Jeff's Monthly Expenses

20% School Supplies

25% Food and Drinks

10% Clothes

10% Bus Fare

35% Computer Games

有一個圓形圖表標示著「傑夫每月花費」。百分之
十是公車費，百分之十是衣服，百分之二十是學校用
品，百分之二十五是飲食，還有百分之三十五是電腦遊
戲。

Question and Test Tip Section

<u>C</u> ❶ **On which two things does Jeff spend an equal amount of money?**
傑夫的花費當中有哪兩項花的錢是相同的？

A. He spends equal money on school supplies and clothes.

在學校用品和衣服方面他的支出一樣多。

B. He spends equal money on bus fare and computer games.

在公車費和電腦遊戲方面他的支出一樣多。

C. He spends equal money on clothes and bus fare.

在衣服和公車費方面他的支出一樣多。

D. He spends equal money on school supplies and computer games.

在學校用品和電腦遊戲方面他的支出一樣多。

解答分析

你找到第一題的關鍵字了嗎？這些字是「兩個」、「事物」和「相等」。這幅圖片以及所有的問題都和「傑夫如何花費」有關，因此你無須注意這些字。現在，你知道"equal"這個字的意思了嗎？equal表示：某些事物有一樣的大小或者數量。

Chapter ❸

解答分析

現在你可以再看一次圖片，然後找出哪兩項是相同的。正確的答案就是這兩項事物。

這種比較類型的題目在英文測試中是很常見的。如果你了解這種句型，那麼答案應該就不難找了。

D ❷ Which of the following statements is correct?
　　下列哪個敘述是正確的？

A. Jeff spends more on bus fare and clothes than on school supplies.
　　傑夫在公車費及衣服上的支出比學校補給多。

B. Jeff spends more on food and drinks than on clothes and computer games.
　　傑夫在飲食方面的支出比衣服及電腦遊戲多。

C. Jeff spends more on clothes than on food and drinks.
　　傑夫在衣服上花的錢比飲食多。

D. Jeff spends more on school supplies and clothes than on food and drinks.
　　傑夫在學校補給及衣服方面的支出比飲食多。

Pictur 3 Race Time ■ ■ ■ ■ ■ ■ ■ ■ ■ ■

賽跑時間

Two Mile Race Finish Times

Aaron	Louise	Dennis	Lauren
12min 40sec	12min 49sec	12min 51sec	13min 07sec

　　這個圖片是一個圖表，顯示四個人完成一次賽跑的速度有多快。此圖表的標題是「兩哩賽跑時間表」。艾倫跑得最快，他以十二分鐘四十秒跑完。路易斯以十二分鐘四十九秒跑完，丹尼斯是十二分鐘五十一秒，而勞倫跑得最慢，花了十三分鐘七秒。

Question and Test Tip Section

<u>C</u> **Who ran slowly compared to Dennis?**
跟丹尼斯比起來誰跑得較慢？

A. Louise ran slowly compared to Dennis.
路易斯跟丹尼斯比起來跑得較慢。

B. Aaron ran slowly compared to Dennis.
艾倫跟丹尼斯比起來跑得較慢。

C. Lauren ran slowly compared to Dennis.
勞倫跟丹尼斯比起來跑得較慢。

D. Nobody ran slowly compared to Dennis.
跟丹尼斯比起來沒有人跑得較慢。

解答分析

第一題利用「比較」這個字要你將所有的跑者和丹尼斯做比較。但是不要被這種類型的句子給混淆了；這些副詞可以在不改變句子語意的情況下，改寫成形容詞的型態。下列句子和第一題所有選項的意思是相同的。

A. Louise ran slower than Dennis.

路易斯跑得比丹尼斯慢。

B. Aaron ran slower than Dennis.

艾倫跑得比丹尼斯慢。

C. Lauren ran slower than Dennis.

勞倫跑得比丹尼斯慢。

D. Nobody ran slower than Dennis.

沒有人跑得比丹尼斯慢。

範例

這個問題是測試你對於**副詞**的了解程度。副詞告訴我們「怎樣、何時、哪裡、為什麼、或者多少」。

Aaron ran quickly.

艾倫跑得很快。

（「快」這個副詞告訴我們艾倫跑得**如何**。）

Aaron ran daily.

艾倫每天跑步。

（「每天」這個副詞告訴我們艾倫**何時**跑步。）

Aaron ran forward.

艾倫向前跑。

（「向前」這個副詞告訴我們艾倫往**哪兒**跑。）

Pictur 4 Weather

天氣

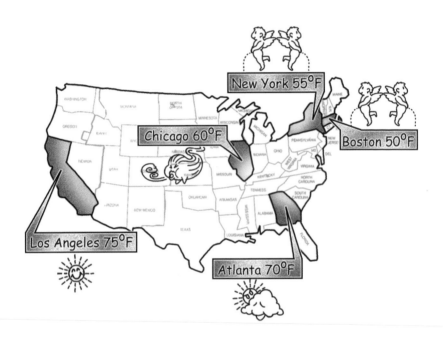

　　這幅圖片是美國的氣候圖。波士頓溫度華氏五十
度、下雨。紐約華氏五十五度、下雨。亞特蘭大華氏
七十度、時陰時晴。芝加哥華氏六十度、多雲。洛杉磯
華氏七十五度、晴天。

Question and Test Tip Section

A ❶ **Which city has the sunniest weather?**
哪座城市的天氣最晴朗？

A. Los Angeles
洛杉磯。

B. Chicago
芝加哥。

C. Boston
波士頓。

D. New York
紐約。

解答分析

這個問題相當簡單。"sunniest"這個字意指「最晴朗」，這叫做**最高級形容詞**。你應該熟知這些不同的形容詞型態以及其字尾。三個主要的形容詞型態是**原級**(sunny)、**比較級**(sunnier)、以及**最高級**（superlative）。例如：

sunny, sunnier, sunniest
晴朗的，更晴朗的，最晴朗的

Chapter **3**

cold, colder, coldest
冷的，更冷的，最冷的

hot, hotter, hottest
熱的，更熱的，最熱的

fast, faster, fastest
快的，更快的，最快的

big, bigger, biggest
大的，更大的，最大的

雖然亞特蘭大和洛杉磯都是晴天，但只有洛杉磯是最晴朗的。因此洛杉磯是正確的答案。

D ❷ Which one of the following statements is true?

下列哪一個敘述是對的？

A. Both Boston and Atlanta are warmer than New York.

波士頓和亞特蘭大都比紐約溫暖。

B. Both Chicago and Los Angeles are warmer than Atlanta.

芝加哥和洛杉磯都比亞特蘭大溫暖。

C. Both New York and Chicago are warmer than Los Angeles.

紐約和芝加哥都比洛杉磯溫暖。

D. Both Los Angeles and Atlanta are warmer than Chicago.

洛杉磯和亞特蘭大都比芝加哥溫暖。

- Better be the head of a dog than the tail of a lion.

（寧為雞首，不為牛後。）

Pictur 5 Tall+Book ■ ■ ■ ■ ■ ■ ■ ■ ■ ■ ■

身高與書本

Daniel　　Monica　　Charles　　Henry

　　圖片上有四個人：一個叫莫尼卡的女孩，拿著三朵花。一個叫丹尼爾的男孩，沒有拿任何東西。一個叫查理斯的男孩，個子最矮，拿著一本書。一個叫亨利的男孩，個子最高，拿著兩朵花。

Question and Test Tip Section

<u>C</u> ❶ **Which one of the following is true about the person holding the book?**
下列有關拿著書的人之敘述哪個是正確的？

A. He is the shortest and his name is Henry.
他的名字叫做亨利，個子最矮。

B. She is also holding a flower and her name is Monica.
她叫做莫尼卡，同時也拿著花朵。

C. His name is Charles and he is the shortest.
他叫做查理斯，個子最矮。

D. Her name is Monica and she is not the tallest.
她叫做莫尼卡，個子不是最高的。

解答分析

這些選項都有兩個獨立的子句。and/or這個字將兩個部分分開。記得要選擇兩個部分都正確的答項。

<u>D</u> ❷ **Which of the following is true about the person, or people, who are holding flowers?**

下列有關拿著花朵的人之敘述哪個是正確的？

A. They are both boys and one of them is the tallest.

他們都是男孩，其中一個最高。

B. Her name is Monica and she is the only person holding a flower.

她叫做莫尼卡，她是唯一拿著花的人。

C. He is a boy and he is not the tallest person.

他是個男孩，而他並非最高的那個人。

D. Their names are Monica and Henry and one of them is the tallest.

他們叫做莫尼卡和亨利，他們其中一人的個子是最高的。

解答分析

又來了，所有的選項都有兩個獨立的部分。練習將這些句子成分分離並且分開閱讀它們。這些答項使用了四個代名詞：「他們」、「她的」、「他的」、以及「他們的」。

Pictur 6 Map

地圖

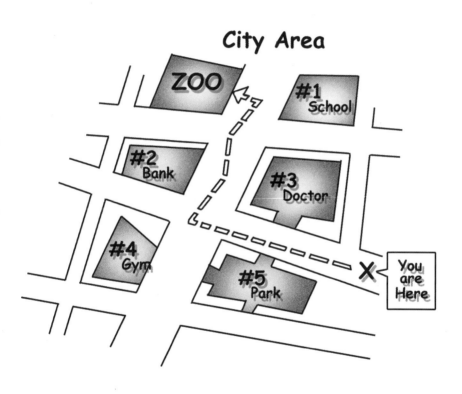

這是一張市區的地圖。"X"這個字母表示「你的位置」，#1表示「學校」，#2表示「銀行」，#3表示「醫院」，#4表示「體育館」，#5表示「公園」。

Question and Test Tip Section

C ❶ **If you are standing on the 'X', which directions would tell you how to get to the zoo?**

如果你站在"X"的位置上，哪一個指示可以告訴你如何到達動物園？

A. First walk straight until you pass the gym, then turn left and walk straight again. The zoo will be in front of you.

首先往前走一直到體育館，接著左轉再往前直走。動物園就在你面前了。

B. First walk straight until you pass the gym, then turn right and walk straight. When you pass the bank turn right and walk straight. The zoo is across from the doctor.

首先往前走一直到體育館，然後右轉再直走。當你經過銀行以後右轉，然後往前直走，動物園就在醫院對面。

C. First walk straight. Before you pass the bank, turn right. Walk straight to the end of the street and turn left. The zoo will be in front of you.

首先往前直走。在你經過銀行以前右轉，直走到那條街的盡頭再左轉。動物園就會在你面前了。

D. First walk straight. Before you pass the bank, turn right. Walk straight until you pass the doctor and then turn left. Walk straight to the end of the street and turn left again. The zoo will be in front of you.

首先往前直走，在經過銀行以前右轉，一直走直到經過醫院後再左轉。走到那條街的盡頭後再次左轉。動物園就會在你面前了。

解答分析

這個問題測試你對方位的熟悉度。你應該已經了解「直的」、「左邊」、「右邊」、「對面」、「前面」、和「經過」這些指示的字詞了。練習將每一組方位指示大聲念出來，同時用你的手指在地圖上跟著指示前進。

- In the country of the blind the one-eyed man is king.
  （比上不足，比下有餘。）

- A little bird is content with a little nest.
  （人窮志短。）

Chapter **3**

<u>D</u> ❷ **If you are standing on the 'X', which of the following statements is true?**
如果你站在"X"的位置，下列哪個敘述是真實的？

A. The bank is closer to you than both the school and the park.

銀行距離你比學校和公園還近。

B. The gym is closer to you than both the zoo and the doctor.

體育館距離你比動物園和醫院還近。

C. The school is closer to you than both the park and the zoo.

學校距離你比公園和動物園還近。

D. The bank is closer to you than both the zoo and the school.

銀行距離你比動物園和學校還近。

解答分析

這個問題要求你做比較。你看到這種類型的比較如何使用「兩者都……」這個字並用以比較兩樣事物嗎？看看下面的例子：

範例

Japan is bigger than both Taiwan and Korea..
日本比台灣和韓國還要大。

→這個句子是正確的,因為日本比這兩個國家的任一個都大。

Japan is bigger than both Taiwan and Canada.
日本比台灣和加拿大還要大。

→這個句子是錯誤的,因為日本雖然比台灣大,但卻沒有比加拿大還要大。Both「兩者都……」這個字在此種比較句型當中意謂著兩個述語當中的任何一個都必須是真實的。

- Friends agree best at distance.
  (朋友之間保持距離,最能契合。)

- Lend your money and lose your friend.
  (借錢給朋友,就失去友誼。)

Pictur 7 Tim's Day

提姆的一天

TiM's Morning Schedule

　　這個圖片的標題是「提姆的早安行程」。圖1顯示時間是早上七點半，提姆正要起床。圖2是早上八點，提姆在吃早餐。圖3是早上八點半，提姆正在開車。圖4是早上九點，提姆正在辦公室內上班。

Question and Test Tip Section

A ❶ When does Tim eat breakfast?
提姆何時吃早餐？

A. Tim eats breakfast before he drives to work and before he starts working.
提姆在開車去上班、在工作以前吃早餐。

B. Tim eats breakfast before he gets out of bed and after he drives to work.
提姆在起床之前、在開車去上班之後吃早餐。

C. Tim eats breakfast after he starts working and before he drives to work.
提姆在開始工作之後、開車去上班之前吃早餐。

D. Tim eats breakfast after he drives to work and before he starts working.
提姆在開車去上班之後、在開始工作之前吃早餐。

A ❷ Which of the following statements about Tim's morning schedule is true?
下列哪個有關提姆早上的行程敘述是真實的？

A. When Tim drives to work, he has already eaten breakfast.
當提姆開車去工作時，他已經吃過早餐了。

Chapter **3**

B. When Tim gets out of bed, he has already driven to work.

當提姆起床時，他已經開車去上班了。

C. When Tim eats breakfast, he has already started work.

當提姆吃早餐時，他已經開始工作了。

D. When Tim eats breakfast, he has already driven to work.

當提姆吃早餐時，他已經開車去上班了。

解答分析

這個問題是測試你是否了解過去時態。"eaten"、"driven"、"started"這些字都是表示過去已經完成的動作。如果你用下列這樣的句型改寫，這些選項的意思也許會更清楚：

A. Tim finished eating breakfast, and then he drove to work.

提姆吃完早餐，然後開車去上班。

B. Tim finished driving to work, and then he got of bed.

提姆開車去上班，然後才起床。

C. Tim finished starting work, and then he ate breakfast.

提姆開始工作以後，才吃早餐。

D. Tim finished driving to work, and then he ate breakfast.

提姆開車去上班後，才吃早餐。

- Better an open enemy than a false friend.
  （明槍易躲，暗箭難防。）

- A friend to all is a friend to none.
  （人盡可友非真友。）

- A man is known by his friends.
  （觀其友，知其人。）

- Short accounts make long friends.
  （帳單短，友誼長。）

- He who has health has hope; and he who has hope has everything.

  （有健康就有希望，而有希望就擁有了一切。）

- The darkest hour is that before the dawn.

  （黎明前的時刻最黑暗。）

- Where there is no vision, the people perish.

  （看不見未來，人就失去生存的意義。）

- He who lives in hope does dance in a hoop.

  （活在希望中的人，就連在鐵環裡也能跳舞。）

- Hope for the best, but prepare for the worst.

  （抱持最大的希望，做出最壞的打算。）

Chapter

4

Appendix 附錄

這句英文，改變你的人生

1

A watched pot never boils.
心急水不沸。

故事分享

任何一件事情未到終局之前，沒有人能夠下定論。同樣的道理，如果一個人因為急於看到結果，往往反而損失慘重。

天才作曲家比才所創作的歌劇《卡門》首演之後，評論極差，這個情況使他終日抑鬱，使他不到一年就氣死了。比才死的時候才三十七歲。令人意外的是，《卡門》卻成為了目前紀錄上演出最多的歌劇。

如果當初比才能夠耐心的等一等，他或許仍有機會可以享受成功的果實，但是他沒有。因為他急於看到成果，因此損失了寶貴的生命。

蘋果電腦的創辦人賈伯斯（Steve Jobs）的經驗，幾乎可以鼓舞所有遭遇困境的人。賈伯斯在大一的時候，曾經感到徬徨困惑，而且對昂貴的學費感到內咎，於是他休學了。二十歲的時候，他發現自己對電腦的熱愛，於是他和朋友史

提夫‧沃克（Steve Wozniak）共同創立了蘋果電腦。

　　剛開始，他們在車庫當中創業，發明許多電腦硬體。公司的成長相當迅速，十年內，營收就成長到二十億美元，擁有四千名的員工。一九八五年，才推出一年而且真正直接銷售給消費者的麥金塔電腦銷售驚人，所以公司的營運可以說是奇佳無比！

　　「然後我就被公司炒魷魚了！」賈伯斯事後在演講中如此說。「怎麼會被自己創立的公司給炒魷魚了呢？」

　　賈伯斯解釋，他們因為找了一位飲料界的高階經理人來管理公司的業務發展，剛開始這位經理人和賈伯斯合作愉快，但是，最後他們倆個意見嚴重分歧，董事會就決定站在新經理人這邊，他們甚至認為，把賈伯斯解雇，對公司才是有利的。

　　三十歲的賈伯斯，就這樣被自己創立十年的公司給掃地出門了。他當時的感受，好像十年來的心血全部都歸無有。

　　賈伯斯經歷了一段自怨自艾、茫然不知所措的時光。然後，他逐漸明白，他不能如此消沉，於是他創

　　立了另一家電腦公司NeXT，還有一家電腦動畫公司皮克斯（Pixar），這段時間，他也戀愛結婚，建立了家庭。之後，更發生令他意想不到的事情：蘋果公司買下了NeXT公

司，再次請賈伯斯回到蘋果電腦，重掌公司經營權。

曾經在對史丹福學生的演講中說到自己的這段經驗：「當時我並沒有察覺。不過，被蘋果炒魷魚，居然成為我這一生中最棒的遭遇。」

如果，賈伯斯不能耐心的面對考驗，面對困境，如果，他無法耐心的等候成功的一天，持續的努力，這一切也不會發生。「心急水不沸」，成功也是如此，只有願意付出耐心，才能有「撥開雲霧見月明」的一天。

賈伯斯癌逝，留下他的座右銘：Stay Hungry, Stay Foolish.(求知若飢，虛心若愚），他以這句名言來勉勵年輕學子。

相關諺語

- Perseverance is sometimes more effective than genius.
  （堅忍有時比天賦更有效。）

- Success belongs to the persevering.
  （成功屬於忍耐的人。）

※ 諺語單字補給站

watched [ˈwatʃt]　被注意著的

pot [pat]　鍋子

boil [bɔɪl]　滾；煮

Perseverance [ˌpɝsəˈvɪrəns]　堅持不懈、忍耐

effective [ɪˈfɛktɪv]　有效的

genius [ˈdʒinjəs]　天資、天賦

belongs [bəˈlɔŋz]　屬於

2

All things come to him who waits.

等待贏得一切。

故事分享

　　心急，是做不好事情的。當你無法耐心等待時，你就不懂得何謂享受人生。

　　有一個年輕人，和女孩子相約見面。當他到了約會的地點時，女孩還沒有到。他只好靠在一棵大樹底下，不耐煩的等著。

　　突然，出現了一個老人。這個老人原來是一個神仙。祂告訴這年輕人：「我知道你在等女孩子，我現在送給你一隻錶，只要你把時針往前快轉，時間就會真的快速的來到你等待的時間。」說完，老人就不見了。

　　年輕人開心的拿起錶，往前快轉一小時，女孩就馬上出現在他的面前了。他和女孩開心的約會著。突然，年輕人想：真想趕快跟她結婚！於是，他又快轉了手錶。

　　一轉眼間，他果然和女孩一起步入禮堂了。接下來，他又想要快點生孩子，又撥快了時鐘，馬上，他身邊就出現了兩個可愛的小嬰孩。他看著可愛的孩子，心想：真希望他們快點長大啊！於是他又撥快了錶。

　　孩子長大、求學、出嫁、也結婚了。這一切都如他所願的，快速的達到了！

　　但是，年輕人突然發現自己已經不再年輕了。因為病痛，他已經躺在床上。床邊的兒孫們和衰老的妻子圍繞著他。老去的年輕人用長滿皺紋的手不停的倒轉著手錶，他不甘的想著：我都還來不及享受人生啊！人生就要結束了嗎？他努力想把時間往回轉。

　　這時候，床邊出現那位老人。老人說：「人生的時間只能往前轉，不能往回轉啊！怎麼樣，你還希望女孩她快點出現嗎？」

　　年輕人一驚，原來，這一切都是一場夢。

　　女孩這時來到了樹下，年輕人一把的把她抱住：「妳來了真好！」女孩問說：「你會等很久嗎？」

　　年輕人開心的回答：「不久！不久！一切都是值得慢慢等待的。」

在這個世界上，耐心誠如鑽石一般，是極為寶貴的品質。有耐心，才可以謙卑，忍耐，克制。有耐心，才不會自大，自負，魯莽。

相關諺語

- Who will go far must go slow.
  （想跑遠的人，必須慢慢的跑。）

- Patience is the best medicine.
  （忍耐是最好的藥物。）

※ 諺語單字補給站

wait [wet] 耐心等待的

medicine ['mɛdəsn̩] 藥物

3

Time will tell.
時間會證明一切。

故事分享

時間，是人生最大的敵人。一切繁華成功，都終究會成為它的灰燼。

就像電影《東邪西毒》中的西毒歐陽峰。他追逐了一生的武林成功，最後，卻也只能自我放逐到大漠十幾年，每天靜靜守著風沙與落日，嘆息的說：「年輕時，總想知道沙漠那邊有什麼，走過去卻發現什麼也沒有，除了沙漠，還是沙漠。」

在無垠的人生沙漠中，我們會企圖完成什麼，我們會想方設法去達到夢想，到最後，很可能一切只是隨風沙飄揚，不留痕跡。

時間會證明一切。你所做的，或許從來就不是新鮮事，對這個宇宙也不曾加添什麼新的觀念，但是，別急。時間會證明一切。

Chapter **4**

久遠的部落時代時，有一個位於高山的部落。部落中有一個年輕人，這個小夥子有一天到外地狩獵的時候，捕獲了一匹野馬。

當他把野馬帶回到部落中，部落裡的每個人讚嘆於野馬的駿美挺拔，並且個個都忌妒這個年輕人，大家都說他一定是一個幸運的男孩。

好景不常，這個男孩為了馴服野馬，不慎被摔下馬背，跌斷了雙腿。於是，族人開始傳說野馬不祥，才會把厄運帶到男孩身上。

行動不便的年輕人只好天天臥病在床，家人也因為害怕野馬帶來的噩運，紛紛走避。

到了兵荒馬亂的時候，部落中的年輕人都被抓去戰場上，只有這個斷了腿的年輕人可以留在家中，免受徵召。這時候，部落中的人又開始傳說，說這匹馬是一匹「良駒」，可以為年輕人帶來幸運。

人生路上的得失與禍福，就在時間的長流中顯得渺小短暫了。因為時間會證實一切，目前看來是禍患的事物，有一天會成為祝福。只要能夠採取這種角度看待一生，我們都能對一時的喜憂處之泰然。「Time will tell.」，挫折又何嘗不是值得感激的呢？

相關諺語

- Procrastination is the thief of time.
  （拖延是時間的賊。）

- Time cures all things.
  （時間能治療一切。）

- Take time when time comes.
  （當時間來臨時，把握時間。）

※ 諺語單字補給站

tome	[taɪm]	時間
tell	[tɛl]	分辨、證實
Procrastination	[proˌkræstəˈneʃən]	拖延
thief	[θif]	賊、小偷
cure	[kjʊr]	醫治

Chapter **4**

4

While there is life, there is hope.

有生命之處，就有希望。／
留得青山在，不怕沒柴燒。

故事分享

在生命的長河中，我們有時候會陷入意料之外的沼澤當中。這時候，不要輕易放棄自己，或者說自己什麼都沒有，只要抱著一個堅定的信念，努力的尋找機會，我們最終會戰勝困境，走出沼澤。

曾經有一位旅行者，企圖穿越沙漠。在沙漠中，他迷失了方向。更可怕的是，他已經吃完了最後一塊乾糧，喝完了最後的一滴水。當他翻遍所有的袋子，他只找到一顆發黃的梨子。

「天哪，我還有一顆梨！」旅行者驚喜的喊叫著。他拿著這顆梨，一腳深、一腳淺的在大漠中尋找出路。整整兩天過去了，他仍然沒有走出廣闊的大漠。飢餓、疲憊卻都一起湧上來。

　　望著茫茫無際的沙海，有好幾次他都想放棄算了。可是，當他看一眼手中的梨，他忍不住用舌頭舔舔乾扁的嘴唇，陡然又添了一些力量。

　　頂著烈日，旅行者艱難的跋涉。終於，數不清跌了多少次，只是每一次他都爬起來，跪著、爬著，彎腰走著，一點點的前進。在他的心中，不斷的默念著：「我還有一個梨，我還有一個梨……」

　　三天之後，旅行者終於走出了大漠。那個他始終沒有咬一口的梨子，已經乾得不成樣子了。他還寶貝似的捧在手中，久久的凝視著。

　　「While there is life, there is hope.（有生命之處，就有希望。）」在越黑暗的角落中，那一點希望的光，就顯得越亮。

相關諺語

- He who has health has hope; and he who has hopehas everything.

  （有健康就有希望，而有希望就擁有了一切。）

- The darkest hour is that before the dawn.
  （黎明前的時刻最黑暗。）

- Where there is no vision, the people perish.
  （看不見未來，人就失去生存的意義。）

- He who lives in hope does dance in a hoop.
  （活在希望中的人，就連在鐵環裡也能跳舞。）

- Hope for the best, but prepare for the worst.
  （抱持最大的希望，做出最壞的打算。）

※ 諺語單字補給站

while	[hwaɪl]	當……的時候
hope	[hop]	希望
darkest	[dɑrkɪst]	最黑暗的
dawn	[dɔn]	黎明
vision	['vɪʒən]	視力、視覺
perish	['pɛrɪʃ]	毀壞、死去
hoop	[hup]	鐵環、箍

5

What the mind can conceive, it can achieve.
心想事成。

故事分享

達文西的手稿畫出全世界第一幅滑翔翼草圖的時候，沒有人想到它真的可能出現。請看一看你的身邊，一切事物剛開始時，都只是一個「想法」。所以，「心想事成」，這並不只是用來祝福別人「萬事順利」，這句話背後真實的意義，是提醒我們「想法」、「創見」何等重要。只要願意去構想、去設計，這一切都是有可能達成的。

一八三四年出生的弗畢綺，她家境貧窮，從小就罹患了關節炎。從小就喜愛植物的她，甚至因此被迫整天留在家中，無法再外出去採植物。

但是，她中學就開始自修，讀了植物學家葛雷的著作《北美植物手冊》，愛不釋手並且收益良多。在一八五八年，哈佛大學成立「植物博物館」時，她央求父母親帶她到波士頓的哈佛大學參觀，她專注站在植物展覽品前面的模樣，引起

博物館館長古岱爾的注意，古岱爾一和她對談，就知道她對植物學的熱愛是哈佛大學植物系無法培養出來的。古岱爾開始每年邀請她來到哈佛大學，特別指導她許多植物知識。弗畢綺因此學到：植物繪畫紀錄，不能只是畫出植物特徵，還必須把植物生長的環境、植物的細膩特徵都畫出來！

之後一八六〇到一八七〇年的十年期間，弗畢綺跟古岱爾學習許多植物標本製作和植物學的知識。一八八一年到一八九五年間，弗畢綺（Kate Furbish）在聖約翰河發現新品種的菊科翠菊「弗畢綺菊」，並證明這種植物的棲地很獨特。

沒有人會想到，這個發現竟然影響到一九七五年美國政府興建大水壩的計畫，美國聯邦政府經過一年的評估，決定保留這個「弗畢綺草」的獨特河岸，否決了水庫建造案。這個案例，成為世界環境保護運動的一個典範。只因為弗畢綺的努力，她影響了近代人類的價值思考：人類是否有權利，消滅一種瀕臨絕種的植物，只為了自己的經濟利益？

心靈，可以帶我們到達所有到的了的遠方目標。阿姆斯壯幼年時，曾經跳躍的對母親說：「我要跳上月球！」在他真正登上月球之前，沒人知道這會真正實現。「What the mind can conceive, it can achieve.」。可見，心想事成並不是祝福人的一句客套話，它是確實可以改造人一生一個信念。

相關諺語

- Work for all you're worth and you'll be worth more.

  （盡你所能，你會更有價值。）

- Human effort can achieve anything.

  （事在人為。）

※ **諺語單字補給站**

mind [maɪnd] 頭腦、智力，心	
conceive [kən'siv] 構想出來	
achieve [ə'tʃiv] 完成，實現	

Chapter 4

6

A brave man smiles in the face of adversity.

勇者不懼。

故事分享

傳聞中，巴爾札克有一枝小枴杖，上面刻著一行字：「我粉碎了一切障礙。」但是，跟他同時代的一個文人，也有一支小手杖，手杖上面卻寫著：「一切障礙粉碎了我。」

同一個年代，不同的勇氣竟然帶來迥異的結果。卡夫卡這一個以《變形記》震撼許多人心靈的作家，就曾經在《卡夫卡書信日記選》當中這麼寫著：

「畏懼就是不幸。但勇氣卻不等於幸福。幸福只是無所畏懼，而不是勇氣。勇氣似乎比力量還強大得多。……所以，不是勇氣，而是無所畏懼，平靜的、直視的，忍受著一切。」

卡夫卡所珍惜的幸福，並不是外人所以為的金錢、名譽、地位和榮耀，他尋求的是一種內心的自由。為了獲得這些真

正的幸福，我們必須懂得如何運用自己的力量。而我們的力量永遠是有限的，因此，我們必須學會放棄，學會忍耐。

一旦遭遇挫折，對許多不曾努力過，也不曾擁有過什麼的人，「放棄」是再簡單不過的一個選擇。但是，一旦放棄了，他們卻只能發現：自己原來根本沒什麼好放棄的。

奧修（Osho）的話是這麼說的：「如果世界仍然吸引著你，如果你覺得還有哪麼一些事情需要去完成，那麼你就要去歷盡那些挫折。你將會感到挫折，那意味著你還需要多逛逛，你還需要誤入歧途。」

勇氣，不是表現得毫不懼怕，而是在非常害怕的時候，卻仍然願意帶著懼意，克服障礙去完成它。

 相關諺語

- He loses indeed that loses last.

  （最後失敗才是真正的失敗。）

- He that can't endure the bad will not live to see the good.

  （無法撐過困境的人，將無法看到好結局。）

※ 諺語單字補給站

brave [brev] 勇敢的

smile [smaɪl] 微笑

face [fes] 面對

adversity [ədˈvɝsətɪ] 逆境，厄運

7

Failure is the mother of success.

失敗為成功之母。

故事分享

　　資生堂，一家在台灣擁有眾多忠實愛好者的化妝品公司。它的創辦人福原有信，是一位經歷過多種考驗，克服許多失敗的成功者。

　　福原有信原本是在海軍醫院的藥局裡面工作，後來他與同事矢野義徹和前田清則同時離職，一起創辦資生堂，經營根據醫師處方箋調藥劑的藥局。

　　不過，生意好的時候，他們三人還可以合作，一旦出現虧損，合夥人之間就容易起爭執。同樣的，早期的資生堂原本看準日本會實施醫藥分業，但是，後來當時的日本政府並沒有馬上實施這種措施。公司立刻陷入困境，於是矢野和前田離開了資生堂，只留下福原繼續經營。

　　不過，失敗為成功之母，「Failure is the mother of success.」，

遭遇挫折之後，福原決定大刀闊斧的改變經營方針。他首先兼賣許多藥品，拓展除了靠處方箋調劑之外的市場。

關鍵的改變是日本的西南戰爭，日本西南戰爭之後霍亂大行，造成藥品需求暴增，所以資生堂因此不斷的茁壯。

一八九七年，資生堂從銀座的小巷子搬遷到大馬路上，開始開設新店，並且販售化妝品。資生堂第一代的化妝品只有三種，分別是化妝水「美膚露」、去污香水「橘花香」、髮油「柳系香」等等。

其中，「美膚露」還是日本著名的藥學專家長井長義從希臘語的「好皮膚」翻譯過來的。這種商品，目前在資生堂的產品目錄當中居然還持續的銷售著！如此長壽的商品，真的是絕無僅有。

一九〇〇年，福原從美國回到日本之後，就開始賣蘇打水和冰淇淋，一九二八年，福原有信過世四年之後，資生堂還在東京鬧區開設了大規模的精品店和藝術餐廳，吸引眾多富豪與仕紳。

誠如資生堂的成長過程，人生，也好比一條崎嶇不平的山路，登上高山的過程中，我們的腳步必須堅穩踏實，我們的目標必須堅定不變，一步一步的努力，才有可能登上山的最高峰。

除此之外，登山的過程也不可能一直都是順利的。成功與失敗，它們往往結伴而來。當前者出現時，我們的生活彷彿煥發光彩，可喜可讚；但當後者出現時，我們往往愁雲慘霧。事實上，失敗並不可悲，因為失敗是創造堅忍毅力的原動力。

「失敗為成功之母」，因為失敗代表的不只是錯誤，因為就算沒有達到目的，在實踐的過程中也會獲得許多原來不知道的智慧和技巧。

愛迪生發明電燈時，不也是在一次又一次的失敗中，終於找到了他所要的燈絲材質，而發明了電燈嗎？不只是愛迪生，所有專家、名人也都是經過了失敗的小徑，自我檢討後再爬起來，才可以邁向成功的高峰。

曾經有一位音樂系的學生，在學音樂的路上遭遇了一連串的挫折。

數不清是第幾次了！這陣子當他走進鋼琴練習室，他總會沮喪的發現：鋼琴上，擺放著一份全新的樂譜。「超高難度……」他無力的翻動著，喃喃自語，感覺自己對彈奏鋼琴的信心似乎跌到了谷底，消磨殆盡。

三個月了，自從跟了這位新的指導教授之後，他不明白，為什麼教授要以這種方式整人？

音樂系學生打起精神，他開始用十隻手指頭奮戰、奮戰，

奮戰琴音蓋住了練習室外教授走來的腳步聲。指導教授是個極有名的鋼琴大師。授課第一天，他就給了自己的新學生一份樂譜。「試試看吧！」他說。

樂譜難度頗高，學生彈得生澀僵滯、錯誤百出。「還不熟，回去好好練習！」教授在下課時，如此叮囑學生。學生練了一個星期，第二週上課時正準備中，沒想到教授又給了他一份難度更高的樂譜。

「試試看吧！」上星期的功課，教授提也沒提。學生再次掙扎於更高難度的技巧戰。第三週，更難的樂譜又出現了，同樣的情形持續著。學生每次在課堂上都被一份新的樂譜剋死，然後把它帶回去練習，接著再回到課堂上，重新面臨難上兩倍的樂譜，卻怎麼樣都追不上進度，一點也沒有因為上週的練習而有駕輕就熟的感覺。

學生的不安、沮喪及氣餒越來越強烈。這一天，教授走進練習室。學生再也忍不住了，他必須向鋼琴大師提出這三個月來、何以不斷折磨自己的質疑。教授沒開口，他抽出了最早的第一份樂譜，交給學生。

「彈吧！」他以堅定的眼神望著學生。不可思議的事發生了，連學生自己都訝異萬分，他居然可以將這首曲子彈奏得如此美妙、如此精湛！教授又讓學生試了第二堂課的樂譜，學生仍出現高水準的表現。

　　演奏結束，學生怔怔地看著老師，說不出話來。「如果，我任由你表現最擅長的部份，可能你還在練習最早的那份樂譜，不可能有現在這樣的程度。」這位教授緩緩地說著。

　　人往往習慣於表現自己所熟悉、所擅長的領域。但，如果我們願意回首，細細檢視，將會恍然大悟的發現——看似緊鑼密鼓的工作挑戰、永無歇止且難度漸升的環境壓力，不也就在不知不覺間、養成了今日的諸般能力嗎？因為，人，確實有無限的潛力！

相關諺語

- Failure is the foundation of success.
  （失敗是成功的基礎。）

- Failure teaches success. （失敗指導了成功。）

※ 諺語單字補給站

failure ['feljɚ]　失敗

success [sək'sɛs]　成功

foundation [faʊn'deʃən]　基礎、基石

8

Great oaks from little acorns grow.

萬丈高樓平地起。

故事分享

心中有大夢想和大目標的人，必須隨時掌握身邊的機會。一個名叫包克的美國年輕人，就因為他願意把握微小的機會，才能完成他的大夢想。

包克幼年的時候就立下了一個夢想：創立一家雜誌。包克立定的目標相當明確，這使得他把握到了一個微不足道的機會。

有一天，包克看到一個人打開一包香菸。從中抽出一張紙條，然後隨即丟到地上。

包克彎下腰，把這張紙條撿起來。那紙條上面印著一個女演員的照片，原來，這是香菸公司為了促銷香菸，從一套照片中挑選出來的一幅照片。包克翻開這張紙片，發現紙片背後什麼都沒有，完全是空白的。包克意識到這是一個機會。

他想：如果把紙片的另一面印上這個演員的小傳記，這種照片的價值就會大大提升。於是，包克找上了印刷這些紙片的印刷廠，向這家公司的經理推銷這個想法。

這個一般人不屑一顧的機會，竟然為包克打開了創業的大道。從此，包克的寫作量大增，越來越多人需要他提供這些演員的小傳記。

慢慢的，包克找來他弟弟和五名編輯，一同寫作小傳，每篇小傳他付了五美元的稿酬給他們，產生的大量小傳專門提供給印刷廠。

沒想到，包克就這樣成為了主編，他最後如願以償成為一家著名雜誌的主編。一個這麼微小的機會被他使用之後，竟然轉變成美好的夢想之樓。

「Great oaks form little acorns grow. （萬丈高樓平地。）」，最能幹的人不是那些等待機會的人，而是那些懂得運用機會、奪取機會、征服機會，讓機會成為自己助力的人。

 相關諺語

- Everything must have a beginning. （萬事皆有起頭。）

- Work has a bitter root but sweet fruit.
  （工作有苦的根，卻有甜的果實。）

※ 諺語單字補給站

oaks [oks] 橡樹們	
acorns ['ekɔrns] 橡子們，橡實們	

Test：看中文重組英文句子。

1. 心急水不沸。(watched A pot boils never)

→ (＿＿＿＿＿＿＿＿＿＿＿＿＿＿＿＿＿＿＿.)

2. 等待贏得一切。(to who All him things waits come)

→ (＿＿＿＿＿＿＿＿＿＿＿＿＿＿＿＿＿＿＿.)

3. 時間會證明一切。(will Time tell.)

→ (＿＿＿＿＿＿＿＿＿＿＿＿＿＿＿＿＿.)

4. 失敗為成功之母。(mother Failure is the of success.)

→ (＿＿＿＿＿＿＿＿＿＿＿＿＿＿＿＿.)

9

Man proposes, but God disposes.

謀事在人，成事在天。

故事分享

飛碟電台、News98電台的董事長趙少康，按照他的人生計畫，他原本不至於走向這個方向。但是，謀事在人，成事在天，上天對他的指引和帶領遠勝於他自己的計畫。

原本一直從政的趙少康，幾年前因為參選台北市長失利，他雖然有四十多萬的選票，但是仍然無法當成市長。敗選之後，趙少康想：「到底我的下一步要做什麼呢？」

趙少康的另一條路，就在此時展開。趙少康曾說：「改行經營電台，那是被迫的選擇。」俗話說，上帝關了你這道門，一定會幫你再開另一扇窗。趙少康果真把飛碟電台、News98經營的有聲有色，飛碟電台年收入曾達到數億之多。

「Man proposes, but God disposes.」，人往往不知道最

適合自己的角色與崗位，直到機緣巧合，把每個人帶到適合
的位置之後，才發生奇妙的成功效果。

相關諺語

- Heaven helps those who help themselves.
  （天助自助者。）

- Heaven never helps the man who will not act.
  （自己不努力，老天也沒轍。）

- When fortune smiles, embrace her.
  （當命運之神向你微笑，請擁抱她。）

※ 諺語單字補給站

propose	[prəˈpoz]	提意見
dispose	[dɪˈspoz]	處理，管理
fortune	[ˈfɔrtʃən]	幸運之神
embrace	[ɪmˈbres]	擁抱

10

No cross, no crown.
吃得苦中苦，方為人上人。

故事分享

《妙媳婦見公婆》這部電影中的艾希莉是這麼說的：「上帝喜歡本來的你，但因為太喜歡了，不能讓你一直那樣。」

這句話，照亮了整部片，輝映了我們的人生。

如果上帝知道我們可以活得精采，活得純真，祂就會利用各種的環境，使我們虛偽的外殼剝落，露出更與祂相近的自己。苦難，因此就成為改變我們的工具。這句「吃得苦中苦，方為人上人」的英文版本：「No cross, no crown.」，直譯出來就是「沒有苦難十字架，就沒有榮耀冠冕。」因此，人生最美的一刻，往往是面對苦難，卻仍然能夠低頭感謝，奮力再起的那一瞬間。

法國大畫家雷諾瓦在晚年的時候得了關節炎，手指頭扭曲變形，每畫一筆，都感受到強烈的劇痛。友人問他：「這麼痛苦，你為什麼還要畫下去呢？」雷諾瓦回答：「痛苦都會

過去，而美麗永存。」

古希臘語當中，「熱忱」的涵義就是指「內心之神」。當一切週遭的環境顯得黑暗、沮喪，當你自我的矛盾強烈得你無法往前，當困難在你的身邊叫囂時，你需要回顧你的「內心之神」，也就是「熱忱」的指引。

演出知名電視劇《宰相劉羅鍋》的李保田，曾經啟發過一個日後身價百萬的股市大師楊教授。這位楊教授原本是唱河南梆子的劇團演員。在劇團中他認識了李保田。在那個人人迷惘的年代中，李保田是最讓他震撼的。當時，不管是劇團內的排演，或者是下鄉演出，李保田總是書不離身。到了1977年恢復高考，全團的人都接到通知，說可以報考中央戲劇學院。但是，最後能考上的，只有李保田一人。幾年之後，李保田成了戲劇學院的教授和知名的電影演員，楊教授卻因為劇團解散，流落到師範學校前面修鞋子。

楊教授當時不願意再錯過人生的失意時刻。他開始旁聽師範學院開的股票投資和證券課程，最後他領悟到徹底改變他命運的一個想法：「股市如人生，不能錯過任何一個低谷。」幾年下來，他成了少數靠暴跌股市卻獲利百萬的證券大師，最後成為大學的教授。

人生確實是如此啊！當命運之神把我們拋到最低谷的地方時，卻是我們投資、進場的最佳時機。在低谷中能夠累積能

量的人，必定能在未來獲得豐厚的回報！

相關諺語

- No gain without pain.
  （一分耕耘一分收穫。）

- Pleasure comes through toil.
  （苦盡甘來。）

- Adversity makes a man wise, not rich.
  （逆境使人長智慧，而非變富有。）

※ 諺語單字補給站

cross	[krɔs]	十字架
crown	[kraʊn]	冠冕

11

When one door shuts, another opens.

天無絕人之路。

故事分享

曾經有人說，別與外界產生任何聯繫，在你的生命中，不應該有任何不能在三十秒內拋棄的東西。生命中，沒有永遠屬於我們的東西。即使是現在顯得如此真實、具體的身體，有一天都會化作塵土，滋養花草。

既然如此，那麼我們何必憑添煩惱呢？當一扇門關了，就讓生命找到另一扇窗吧！

蕭宇超，台灣政治大學的語言學教授，他從小就是小兒麻痺，只能成天坐在輪椅上，沒辦法自由行動。但是，他在語言學界成立語言學會，設計語言計算公式，利用輸入（Input）、輸出（Output）的分析方式，分析出語句中的特殊用詞，並且作育英才，影響無數學子。

美國自由車手蘭斯．阿姆斯壯，他七歲就開始騎自行車，

童年時候，他甚至從德州一路上騎到奧克拉荷馬州，最後甚至要他的母親開車來接他。

蘭斯在成年之後，不斷的參加自行車競賽，在他25歲那一年，他已經是全世界排名第七的車手了。蘭斯正過著一個多麼風光的精采人生時，上帝卻在此時關了他的一扇窗。

當時蘭斯感到非常的疲倦和虛弱，經醫生檢查，他已經得到了癌症，而且蔓延到腦部，存活率只有40%。在看似絕望的人生中，蘭斯卻能努力的對抗病魔，並且在1998年，終於能夠再參加康復後的第一場比賽。一比賽，他就奪得了環法比賽的冠軍。

蘭斯用他康復後的一生，不斷的打敗來自世界各地的自行車手，在他退休之後，蘭斯仍然努力的為了募集癌症獎金而在全世界奔走著。

「When one door shuts, another opens.」只要一扇門關了，另一扇門就會開啟。因此，我們毋須哭泣，因為天使的腳步聲總在困境之時和孤單之夜，顯得特別清晰！

 相關諺語

- When things are at the worst they begin to mend. （苦盡甘來。）

- Look on the bright side.
  （凡事往好處看。）

※ 諺語單字補給站

shuts [ʃʌt] 關上	
another [ə'nʌðɚ] 另一個，再一個	

12

A bad penny always comes back.

惡有惡報。

故事分享

有三個人被關進監獄三年。這三個人一個是美國人，一個是法國人，一個是猶太人。典獄長為了表示寬容，答應滿足他們三人一人一個要求。美國人愛抽煙，他就要求典獄長給他煙。法國人愛浪漫，他就要求要有美女相伴。猶太人則對典獄長說：「請給我一部可以與外界溝通的電話。」

三年過去了，他們都要出獄了。美國人首先衝出來，鼻子上塞滿了香菸，邊跑邊大叫著：「給我火！給我火！」原來，他只記得要煙，忘了要火。

法國人則是兒女成群，手牽著俏佳人一起出來了。

猶太人最後一個走出監獄，出來時，他緊緊握著典獄長的手：「太感謝你了。這三年中，我靠著電話與外界聯繫，生意不但沒有中斷，還成長了200%，為了報答你，我馬上送你

一台勞斯萊斯。」

上面的小故事或許看來有點好笑、有趣，但是卻啟示了「選擇」的重要性。知名電影《蜘蛛人》裡，也有一段與「選擇」有關的情節。

年輕的蜘蛛人彼得‧帕克為了購買中古車討好暗戀的女孩MJ，他到了摔角場打工。

成功打敗摔角選手的他，卻被摔角場老闆騙了，只拿到100美元的報酬，而不是原先約定的3000美元。為了要報復摔角場老闆，彼得放走搶劫了摔角場老闆的搶匪。沒想到，這個搶匪隨即殺死扶養他長大的班叔叔。

彼得不斷回想起那短短一瞬間的機會，他能攔下這個搶匪，如果他選擇站在公義這一邊，而不是報仇這一邊，他的叔叔也許就不會死亡了。因為這個衝擊，彼得開始他打擊犯罪的「正義蜘蛛人」生涯。

什麼樣的選擇，就導致什麼樣的生活。我們今日的生活是肇因於三年前所做的選擇，甚至前一秒鐘所做的選擇，也會影響未來。就在今天，我們已經決定了明天。「A bad penny always comes back.（惡有惡報。）」，當然好事也有好報。人世間的善與惡的循環，就是如此彼此牽連著。

 相關諺語

- Good for good is natural, good for evil is manly. （以德報德很自然，以德報怨則是大丈夫。）

※ 諺語單字補給站

bad [bæd] 不好的，壞的

always [ˈɔlwez] 總是，經常

penny [ˈpɛnɪ] 便士，一便士硬幣

back [bæk] 回來

13

History repeats itself.

歷史會重演。

故事分享

　　社會上哪有任何事不能用波段解釋呢？作家第一次的作品，有可能沉睡在倉庫中多年，沒有人賞識，但是一轉眼，他又可能因為某個事件出名，使他的作品大大暢銷。在太陽底下，哪有新鮮事呢？曾經流行過長裙，短裙退流行；一轉眼，短裙又流行了起來。曾經流行過格子狀的布紋，一轉眼又變成條紋狀的布紋較流行。相信我，過沒多久，妳會看到格子狀的布紋又大受歡迎。

　　已經發生的事情，後面一定會再發生的。成功歷程，絕對不是獨特的，而是有許多相似的環節。歷史就是如此，一直不斷的重複著。

　　既然歷史是不斷的重複的，處於歷史長流中的你我，該如何應對，如何自處？

　　我們該在面對成功時微笑，在失敗的時候更開懷的笑。因

為歷史總是會重複的，只要能熬過這一個階段，成功的浪潮會再次沖向你。

相關諺語

- There is nothing new under the sunshine.
  （太陽底下沒有新鮮事。）

※ 諺語單字補給站

history	[ˈhɪstərɪ]	歷史
repeat	[rɪˈpit]	重複
itself	[ɪtˈsɛlf]	它自己

14

Look before you leap.
三思而後行。

故事分享

　　早期的美國阿拉斯加，是個冰天雪地的地方。那時，有一個年輕夫婦，妻子難產後留下一個孩子，丈夫一面必須出外求生活，無法照顧孩子，所以就訓練了一隻狗，幫忙照顧孩子。

　　這隻狗聰明聽話，不但會咬著奶瓶餵奶給孩子喝，還會看家。

　　有一天，主人外出了，叫狗照顧孩子。他卻在別的鄉村被大雪攔阻，當天沒辦法趕回家。第二天，他趕緊回到家中，一開門，狗就出來迎接主人。但是當他把房門打開，卻只見到到處是血，床上也是血，孩子不在身邊。而這隻狗卻滿口血跡。主人以為牠狗性發作，咬死了孩子。大怒之下，拿起刀向著狗頭一劈，把狗殺了。

　　之後，他卻突然聽到孩子的聲音。床底下一個孩子爬出

來。這時候他才注意到那條死了的狗大腿的肉都被咬掉了。
而房間的角落也躺著一匹嘴上還咬著狗肉的狼。

原來，他不在家的夜晚，這隻狗救了小主人，卻被誤殺了。
這真是何等可悲的誤會！

　　誤會就是在人不了解、不理智、無耐心的時候發生的。感
情極度衝動的時候，如果我們能夠「三思而後行」，先看清
楚再行動，有多少悲劇會被挽回啊！

相關諺語

- Draw not your bow till your arrow is fixed.
  （除非架好箭，否則別拉弓。）

- Think before you act.
  （行動之前考慮好。）

- Think today and speak tomorrow.
  （今天想清楚，明天說出口。）

- Think twice before you do.
  （採取行動之前先反覆想。）

※ 諺語單字補給站

look [lʊk] 看

before [bɪ'for] 在……之前

leap [lip] 跳躍

draw [drɔ] 拉開、引出

arrow ['æro] 箭

fix [fɪks] 架好、架牢

twice [twaɪs] 兩次

15

Nothing comes of nothing.
事出必有因。

故事分享

發明心臟導管手術的女性醫學家道希葛，她在一九六二年，因為福爾摩斯的精神，阻止了更多畸形胎兒的誕生。

當時，道希葛在德國的學生貝優蘭來拜訪她，學生告訴她一個驚人的數據：德國當時出現了一種稱為「海豹肢」的畸形兒。

這些畸形兒一出生的時候，智力與正常兒童無異，但是下肢卻像海豹一樣，長不出下肢來。一九五九年，海豹肢的病例有十二個，到了一九六〇年，竟然增加到二十六個案例。

貝優蘭原本以為這是環境污染的結果，但是速度增加之快，讓人懷疑。到了一九六二年，海豹肢的畸形兒案例已經增加到上千名。

細心的貝優蘭還發現，這些畸形兒的母親，在懷孕期間都服用了一種名為「沙利竇邁」的止吐劑。這種止吐劑是大藥廠

的產品，聲稱不會有副作用，可以解決懷孕婦女害喜的問題。

道希葛立刻覺得問題嚴重，她飛到德國，並且在當地找到一位醫生協助她做實驗，並且發現：沙利竇邁會抑制胎兒骨細胞的發育。

道希葛立刻發表文章，呼籲孕婦應該立即停用這種藥物。消息公開之後，雖然挽救了許多畸形兒童，但是一九六二年年底，海豹肢的嬰兒仍然達到了上萬名。

「Nothing comes of nothing.」，任何一件事的發生，背後都有隱藏的原因。但是往往人們無法敏感的察覺到「找出原因」的重要性，錯過了搶救危機的關鍵時刻。

相關諺語

- No smoke without fire. （無風不起浪。）

- Every why has a wherefore. （事出必有因。）

※ 諺語單字補給站

come [kʌm] 來自於

of [ɔv] 屬於

16

There are two sides to every question.

公說公有理，婆說婆有理。

故事分享

任何一件事情，都會引發兩種截然不同的想法。

有一個年輕人來到了一個綠洲。在這個綠洲中有一位老人，年輕人問：「這裡如何呢？」老先生反問他：「你的家鄉如何呢？」年輕人回答說：「糟透了！我很討厭那！」老人家接著說：「那你趕快走，這裡和你的家鄉一樣糟糕。」

接著，又來了一個年輕人。同樣的，這個年輕人詢問老人：「這裡如何呢？」老人也問他同樣的問題。年輕人回答說：「我的家鄉很好，我很想念家鄉的人、事、物……」老人家就說：「那麼這裡也是一樣那麼好！」

面對同一個問題，同一個地點，老年人卻有迥異的回答。這就好像這句名言所說的：「There are two sides to every question.」

　　我們可以選擇從正面的角度看事情，也可以選擇從負面的角度看事情。而我們在爭議任何一個問題的時候，難免會有一些對立的看法。

　　在每一個爭執的背後，都隱藏著一個偏執：我的看法比他的看法高。他的看法比不上我的。這些偏執觀念引發的戰火，不斷在同事、親人、夫妻、朋友當中燃燒。

　　因此，真正徹底除去爭執的方式是：「看別人比自己強。」把對方的優點與長處時常記憶在心中，不管對方是否真的做錯，提出意見的時候，永遠先讚美對方。

 **相關諺語**

- Every advantage has its disadvantage.
  （有利必有弊。）

- Every white hath its black, and every sweet its sour.
  （有白必有黑，有甜必有酸。）

※ 諺語單字補給站

side [saɪd] 立場	
question ['kwɛstʃən] 問題	
hath [hæθ] 有，has的古字	

Test：看中文意義，重組英文單字，寫出完整的名句。

1. 吃得苦中苦，方為人上人。(crown No cross, no)

→ (＿＿＿＿＿＿＿＿＿＿＿＿＿＿＿＿.)

2. 天無絕人之路。(another one opens door When shuts,)

→ (＿＿＿＿＿＿＿＿＿＿＿＿＿＿＿＿.)

3. 惡有惡報。(A always bad comes penny back)

→ (＿＿＿＿＿＿＿＿＿＿＿＿＿＿＿＿.)

4. 歷史會重演。(repeats History itself)

→ (＿＿＿＿＿＿＿＿＿＿＿＿＿＿＿＿.)

17

The more, the better.
多多益善。

故事分享

人生有幾件事情是不嫌多的：讀書不嫌多、朋友不嫌多、經驗不嫌多。擁有夠多的知識和資訊，就等於擁有豐富的商機；朋友一牛車，就能讓結成網的人脈，成為自己的成功基礎。經驗累積得夠多，面對考驗就能隨手取得解決方法，時機一對，過去的經驗就能幫助我們掌握成功關鍵時刻。所以說「The more, the better.（多多益善。）」，多多益善，上述三種改變人生的成功要素，是任何一個成功人士無法否認的。

85度C的董事長吳政學，就是個朋友不嫌多、經驗不嫌多的成功創業人。台灣知名財經商業雜誌《今週刊》就曾經對他做過特別專訪。

雲林縣口湖鄉人吳政學，對童年的經驗就是不斷的轉學。國小時，他的父母親為了尋求更好的發展機會，從雲林老遠來到三重，又落腳在豐原。吳政學國中畢業時就到外島當

兵。即將退伍前夕，父母親仍然存不夠錢買房子，甚至為了買房子的事情有爭執。看到父母親的影子的吳政學，為了脫離貧窮，不斷的閱讀部隊裡面大專兵買來的管理雜誌，這可以說是他一輩子書讀得最多的時候。

一九八九年退伍時，當時一家豐原的網球工廠正在應徵員工，吳政學選擇了論件計酬的計件員。別人五點下班，他做到半夜十二點。短短三個月，他就累積了人生第一桶創業金十二萬元。

吳政學對排隊這件事情特別敏感。只要一看到有人龍，他就一定會仔細思考原因，並且從市場當中蒐集機會。他注意到自己常去的理髮廳中，有一個理髮師傅特別熱門，客戶總是大排長龍。因此，當這位理髮師傅提到附近有黃金店面出租時，吳政學立刻邀請他出來創業。

專業的理髮師傅成為他的得力助手。短短五個月，他們就開了第二家分店。重複著洗頭、招呼客人的日子一年之後，吳政學開始尋找新的契機。他轉行經營鞋廠、大理石舖石工作，經歷了鞋廠工業外移、營建產業沒落的危機，敏銳的吳政學追浪追得快，抽身也抽得快。他開始到處拜訪朋友，聊天、找機會，他知道做生意不能死守空頭。

一九九七年，吳政學發現他當兵時的同袍郭文河在東海大學旁的泡沫紅茶店「休閒小站」生意很好，老是有人排隊。

他又投入休閒小站的連鎖經營。

吳政學豐富的經驗並不一定都是成功的。吳政學看到休閒小站的連鎖商機之後，企圖自創品牌「Pizza Hot熱到家」，一開始業績爆紅，但是第三個月卻業績反轉直下。因為這段失敗經驗，吳政學之後的創業顯得更加審慎。

二〇〇四年，吳政學觀察到一點：即使是在SARS風暴之下，五星級飯店的便當還是很多人排隊搶著要。可見民眾對「五星級」出品的餐點特別嚮往，他從這個小細節找到了商機。抓住「五星級」創業的焦點，吳政學找到了四大五星級糕點名師之一的鄭吉隆做搭檔，創辦了知名的85度C。這次的創業，就像他當初邀請理髮師傅創業一樣，因為找對專家，成果當然驚人。

五星級的糕點，卻以平價銷售，而且吳政學這次採用中央廚房，統一配送，避免「熱到家」各家口味不統一的品質控管難題，成功攻佔飲品與咖啡市場。

回顧吳政學的一生，他擁有豐富的創業經驗，多多益善的人脈，以及專業的知識。他的成功應證了「The more the better.」這句名言。經驗越多，人脈越多，知識越多，對創業絕對是有利無害的！

 相關諺語

- Reading enriches the mind.
  （閱讀豐富了心靈。）

- An old man's sayings are seldom untrue .
  （老人的經驗難得出錯。）

※ 諺語單字補給站

more [mor] 較多的
better [bɛtɚ] 較好的

18

Better bend than break.
識時務者為俊傑。

故事分享

在馬倫哥戰役當中，奧地利的軍隊被法國軍隊擊敗。當時，奧地利的指揮官馬可將軍被俘擄，囚於法國。然而，有一天，他趁著戒備鬆懈之時逃跑了。當拿破崙的部下忐忑不安的將此事報告給拿破崙時，拿破崙卻說：

「他沒有帶副官，就這麼隻身逃跑了？」拿破崙的部下回答說：「是的，他隻身一人。」

拿破崙立刻說：「馬上打發他的副官也隨同去吧。這麼顯要的人，沒有隨從隻身獨行是不成體統的。這位將軍以後對我們還有用。」

後來，到了1805年的戰爭剛開始的時候，馬可將軍就在烏爾姆威城下，率領大批奧地利軍隊投降拿破崙。

真正的英雄，面對時勢改變的時候，是不會堅持己見，反而懂得看穿時勢，暫時放手。

拿破崙是識時務的人，因為他能用敏銳的目光，透過深思，不被眼前的狀況所侷限，總是看得很遠、很遠，有如山鷹，從遼遠的高山中，就能看到低谷的獵物。

所謂「時勢造英雄，英雄造時勢」，拿破崙退一步，　把馬可將軍的副官也放了，　就是稍微「彎（bend）」了自己的身分，願意在馬可將軍面前稍微讓步。這豈不是遠比派兵去追捕，「破壞（break）」馬可將軍的信心更來得聰明嗎？

「Better bend than break.（ 識時務者為俊傑。）」，只要懂得審度時勢，任何環境都可以是扭轉困境的好機會。

以台灣政界的許多政治人物從政歷程看來，很多人都是先彎腰、失敗之後，然後才獲得成功的。所謂「哀兵必勝」，在台灣引起諸多爭議的總統陳水扁，縱然評價兩極，他的從政歷程卻也應驗了這句話：「Better bend than break.（識時務者為俊傑。）」。

陳水扁在台北市長參選落敗之後，轉戰2000年的總統一職，他以些微的差距獲得成功。因為他利用敗選的演講鼓舞支持民眾，塑造出悲壯的犧牲形象。

當時，有許多政治觀察家一見到他選後的表現，立刻就預測到：「這段演講太好了，如果是選舉前講，一定能贏得不

少票數。」果然，2000年的總統大選中，陳水扁出乎意料的當選了。

可惜，陳水扁在連任二屆總統時，因海角七億，貪污事件，被判刑，導致身敗名裂，而鋃鐺入獄，現在已經被關了四年多，最近又因疑似帕金森症，是否再回北監，而鬧得沸沸揚揚，遺憾一生。

寧可彎腰累積躍起的能量，不要長久保持高姿態，最後卻被一次折斷。寧可低頭尋找下一次機會，也不要永遠昂首而被困境痛擊。

「Better bend than break.」並不僅是對人生以及事業的提醒，在人際交往上面，又何嘗不是如此呢？能夠低姿態的尋求和平，就是成功了。

相關諺語

- Better a living beggar than a buried emperor.
  （寧願活著當乞丐，也不要死了稱王。）

- The best fish swims near the bottom.
  （好魚總是在底部游。／有價值的東西，必須艱難努力才能拿到。）

- The higher up, the greater the fall.
  （爬得愈高，摔得愈慘。）

※ 諺語單字補給站

bend [bɛnd] 彎曲，使彎曲

break [brek] 折斷

英語系列：24

英語聽力滿分特訓

主編／施銘瑋
作者／Craig Sorenson
譯者／吳佳燕
出版者／哈福企業有限公司
地址／新北市中和區景新街 347 號 11 樓之 6
電話／(02) 2945-6285　傳真／(02) 2945-6986
郵政劃撥／31598840　戶名／哈福企業有限公司
出版日期／2016 年 3 月
定價／NT$ 249 元（附 MP3）

全球華文國際市場總代理／采舍國際有限公司
地址／新北市中和區中山路 2 段 366 巷 10 號 3 樓
電話／(02) 8245-8786　傳真／(02) 8245-8718
網址／www.silkbook.com　新絲路華文網

香港澳門總經銷／和平圖書有限公司
地址／香港柴灣嘉業街 12 號百樂門大廈 17 樓
電話／(852) 2804-6687　傳真／(852) 2804-6409
定價／港幣 83 元（附 MP3）

視覺設計／Wan Wan
內文排版／Jo Jo
email ／ haanet68@Gmail.com

郵撥打九折，郵撥未滿 500 元，酌收 1 成運費，
滿 500 元以上者免運費

國家圖書館出版品預行編目資料

英語聽力滿分特訓 / 施銘瑋◎主編 Craig Sorenson◎ 著
.吳佳燕◎譯 -- 新北市：哈福企業, 2016.03
　　面；　公分. -- (英語系列；24)
　　ISBN 978-986-5616-48-9(平裝附光碟片)

1.英語 2.讀本

805.18　　　　　　　　　　　　　　105002317

哈福